# ENCORE APARTMENTS L.A.

## The Tiffany Orr Mystery

### LEWIS BYRD

No part of this book may be reproduced or transmitted in any form or by any means, electronic or mechanical, including photocopying or recording, or by any information storage and retrieval system, without permission in writing from the author. However, excerpts from this book may be quoted in reviews without prior permission.

contact: fanfares@juno.com

copyright © 2018 Lewis Byrd

On the cover:
Photo from William Reagh Collection,
Los Angeles Public Library

p 3

All rights reserved.

ISBN-10:1727097696
ISBN-13:978-1727097696

For Daffy

ENCORE APARTMENTS

# CHAPTER 1

Another bright Los Angeles morning prodded April up from another lazy sleep, a sleep unburdened by having to get up and rush off to work. She loved the unemployment checks, if only they would last forever. She loved the free rent she was now getting as the new manager of Encore Apartments—if only the couple at war with each other upstairs did not blow themselves and the building up before they could be evicted. And she loved the pink boxes of donuts that her new boyfriend, Jerry, had been dropping off—if only he were a little more exciting.

Nonetheless, she bounced out of bed. Life is good! Life is glorious, she sang to herself, springing onto her feet with a heart full of giggles, ready to take the day.

And then the music went from major to minor. That vacant unit across the hall from where the two loud ones lived. If only April Downing could find somebody to rent it. This would be her first rental, technically as trial manager. In fact, she did not at all love having to interview total strangers. So far, applications were not looking good. Why had so many young star-struck crazies and drugged-out "musicians" applied? Too flaky for me, thought April. Were there no qualified adults out there? The few who had applied looked more like out-of-work extras seeking Section Eight rates. Most people who could afford regular rates were looking for a one bedroom, not a studio, thank you, however glamorous the area and the old building's reputation. April would check with Manny across the hall, who served as a backup when the manager was out, to see if he'd had any queries the previous day when she was in Glendale at the party with Jerry.

She decided to try feeling flattered by her new boyfriend, who worked in a bakery, even if she felt only a faint spark.

A sudden jolt from above pulled her back into the reality of managing: Not those two loonies going at it again, she thought. Or were they rehearsing a scene this early in the morning? The creeps! Only a week earlier, Cecil in Unit 9, known for dramatizing any incident he could run with, had anxiously reported having heard a gunshot across the hall. Since there had been only one "gunshot," April calmed him down a little, and then Manny, appearing at Cecil's door, suggested it might have come from the house on the south side of the building. However, between themselves, April and Manny were not so sure, wondering if the Loud Ones upstairs had armed themselves.

April waited for another jolt. Nothing. Relief. She was thinking that by the time her unemployment checks ran out, maybe the May Company would hire her back, as it had promised, expecting a slump in business to turn. Or, maybe by then she would have landed a solvent man to sweep her off her feet, and cure her of her money worries. Jerry was halfway on her mind. He was not the type to sweep a woman off her feet, and probably another reason why April should take this new boyfriend of hers, Jerry, more seriously. If only he were a little more, what? Rough on the edges. Well, Jerry held down a steady job, and that should put him at the front of her brain. Too many of the men she went for were either needy or greedy, "in between" jobs, and she had felt serially taken advantage of. Enough!

Life is good! Life is glorious! she repeated, walking over to a small mirror on the fridge, where life could be brutal --- with her eyes wide open. Not too bad, she thought, turning her profile to study the roundness of her thick neck. Any less thick? She used "thick" a lot, instead of "fat." Had she lost a few pounds? The mirror did not lie, except when April stood in front of it. She decided to believe that her figure was less thick. And so she felt lighter on her feet, and decided to indulge in another donut from the large pink box that Jerry had given her, after driving her home from the party in Glendale. It had marked their first date. The fact that they even considered it their first date was itself a good sign. They had only known each other casually for a couple of months, and now they had taken what Jerry called "the first step." To April, it felt more like a first minuet, it was so virginal. She still had a hot bartender up in the Valley English equestrian center on her otherwise blank dance card.

At the end of one donut, she dug into a second, all of the remaining ones seeming to cry out, "Take me, please!"

"No! No! No!" her adult mind cried, as she often conversed with food. Over a couple of days, April had consumed nearly half the box. Oh, God, she groaned, I've got to reduce way down and prepare for old age. Just a cup of coffee. Not another pastry. Give them up. Tell him why. He's trying to seduce me through sugar. But by the time he gets me between his sheets, there won't be enough room for both of us.

Jerry worked at a bakery in Glendale, and his good-guy solidity appealed to April when she was in one of her I-hate-flaky-men moods. She'd been stood up two nights earlier by a hard rock musician, himself not the most toned of LA mortals. Out, damn desire! shouted April to the box, slamming the lid shut.

She crossed to the front door and went out to make her daily rounds. "Keep an eye always open," said the property owner, Alex, after he had asked her to manage on a trial basis following the abrupt departure of the previous manager, Leila, whom everyone had seemed to like. Alex could rely, as well, on the volunteer services of the charming gadabout Manny, a long-term resident who dwelled contentedly in the small studio across the hall from April. Manny had been a musician in better days. Now he enjoyed poking about the premises and reporting back to "management" on suspicious activity. Since Manny was usually around, when the manager was away, on occasion he would handle minor complaints, like leaky faucets or constipated toilets, and take rental applications. For this, his rent had not been raised in over ten years. Alex was charmed by Manny, but he could not see the aging Aussie managing the thirteen units.

April and Manny had become good friends. The huge age difference made it possible, for Manny would never make a pass. April would wait for another hour or so before asking Manny if anybody had dropped by the day before to fill out an application for the still-vacant studio on the second floor, just across from the Loud Ones. Anyway, if he was up by now, Manny was probably out taking his morning walk down to Wilshire, where a little café and a copy of the Los Angeles Times gave him a perfect Sunday morning.

Through the staid heirloom fragrance of the locally famed apartment house, April sauntered up the stairs to the second floor, feeling happily in charge. And then, feeling a charge of unprofessional lust, she hovered slowly as she passed unit 10. The Loud Ones. They were Wayne Rank, who worked as a delivery man for a warehouse in Inglewood, and his "actress" girlfriend, a natural born vixen (in her mind), Melissa Cusp. They had come out to Los Angeles from New Jersey, a couple of years before. Rank wanted to be a stunt man, only to find the work as hard to come by as were acting jobs for Melissa, who so far had not managed to snare a single role in anything. Not even a commercial. They produced a lot of ominous sounds up there, and Alex was wanting to be rid of them. April and Manny were banking on some big incident they could use to launch an eviction.

But Wayne had a body that caused April's cinematic brain to cast her and him in wild scenes of abandon. He had a face of bark and brawn that sent shivers down her thick spine. She knew he was fire, but still secretly hoped that the door would open when she happened to be passing by, and he would come out of it and say something that she could work with. She was praying for a backed-up toilet or gas fumes from the heater in there to plague his apartment and necessitate his calling the in-house manager. Anything to give her quality time in front, *directly in front of*, the irresistible stud.

The second floor was harder to handle. Across the hall from where Wayne and Melissa rehearsed, vacant Unit 11's last occupiers had been a couple of strange brothers, who kept to themselves, but through whose front door came and went an eerie parade of young pimply things, who might have been on drugs or on parole, or both. In fact, many tenants believed that Leila had been fired for renting to the brothers. When finally evicted, they left behind a bathtub sprouting living things of the freaky sort one may come upon in a novel by Stephen King. This was the infamous unit, rumored to be jinxed, for which April was seeking the first renter on her "trial" watch. She took the opportunity to go inside and look around, really, to stare through the peep hole in the door, hoping to catch a glimpse of Wayne coming or going. Get a grip, girl! she told herself, pulling back. She crossed the room to look into the kitchen, thinking of the baker boy.

April wanted to impress Alex, of course. Alex lived up in the Valley, and hardly ever came around. He had made a fortune as a Hollywood agent. And then his aura faded as he was aced out by larger agencies stealing away his A-list clients, leaving him with an aging roster of provisional has-beens. If he could book one at least into the green room at the Johnny Carson Tonight Show, there to be passed over night after night until they gave up, or died — that was a score for Alex. So he had wisely invested in real estate. He owned five other apartment houses, and he operated them in hands-off fashion, relying on his on-site managers to handle most of the business. He only got involved on major issues, such as the recent messy bathtub eviction, as they called it.

April came out of the kitchen and went to the back window. And looked out ... down there stood a strange man in the driveway, looking up. She wondered what he was doing. Maybe checking out the place before applying. She crossed to the front door to leave, but stopped short, hearing familiar voices across the hall.

"Scum bag! I took Grant's offer!"

Silence.

April froze. Melissa's voice, or was it?

"I could make your life a living hell!"

Please do try. Maybe you'll give me a rise I am not getting from you in any other way!"

"Bitch!"

"Getting better, Wayne!"

Wayne. She heard Wayne. They must be acting.

"Read the thing right!"

"A living hell," bellowed Wayne.

Laughing..

Sure, that's what they were doing, concluded April, with relief.

She let go of her compulsion and walked back down the hall, and downstairs. Let them kill each other. Anything to expedite their removal.

Another unsettling bolt visited Encore Apartments.

An earthquake?

April stopped at the foot of the stairs. She heard a noisy car outside, probably along the driveway, roaring off. Maybe it had caused the fleeting shake.

She stopped before going into her apartment, deciding to first pay a visit to Manny across the hall, to see what he might have heard. She knocked on his door.

Moments later, it opened up, and his crinkled face, which bore a comical resemblance to the puppet Punch, appeared.

Good morning, April," he yawned.

"Did I wake you, Manny?"

"No, of course not. Already took me walk. What's up, anything good?"

"You didn't hear a loud crash?"

"Oh, yeah, I thought maybe another little earthquake on a call-back from Universal."

April giggled. "Oh, that's what it was. I'd heard them acting up there on my rounds."

"Drama queens, both," said Manny.

"Him too?"

Manny grinned. "Who knows? I could tell you things about this town. If I were you, I'd stick to the baker boy, girl." Was that a hint from Manny?

"How did the party go?"

April stalled. How to put a spin on it. "I guess okay, for a first date."

"No sizzle?"

"He's, well, a nice guy."

"That's all"

April smiled. "We'll see." Changing the subject, "Any more applications, from yesterday?" she asked.

"We did get one, a good one, I think. At last. I was going to show you. She came by last evening when you were out. Sit down. I'll get it."

Manny crossed to a small book shelf

April dropped into a small leather couch that had been self-shredding for years.

"A woman, middle age, charming."

"Middle age, yes!" said April.

Manny was still thinking about April's love life. "So nothing romantic, aye?"

"I don't know. I didn't feel many sparks."

"Give it time. You rush into these things too fast."

"How well you know me."

"I'd take a baker over a bartender any day," said Manny, shuffling through a pile of papers on the top of a small bookcase. The room was darkened by the shades being drawn. It always felt a little too gloomy in there for April. Maybe he kept the shades down because the windows looked out onto a driveway across from the white building, and he didn't like people stealing glances of his humdrum existence. The room was furnished with old pieces. The bookcase was stuffed with books he had probably never read.

April wondered if this would one day become her lot. Her father told her to appreciate time spent with older people, for in their lives she could learn to understand what likely lay ahead for herself.

"And how's the job search, April?"

"I prefer working for the State of California."

"Good hours?"

"I go out on the off hours, slipping applications under closed doors and into mail boxes, and keeping a list, so I can show the unemployment people that I've been out looking."

Manny smiled. "Well, you've been out, at least. I know the charade well." He handed April the application. "You're the boss. Tell me how this one looks to you."

April looked it over.

"Tiffany Orr."

"Speaks well. Has a good winning way."

And Manny is attracted, thought April.

"Tiffany Orr," she repeated, an instant disbeliever in the name. "Sounds made up."

"Most of them are."

"Is yours?"

"Manny Sheffield. How could that be made up?"

They laughed.

. "Why do we have to go through so many of these to find a risky one we feel good about?"

"She might be the one. Educated, must be."

To himself, Manny was running the applicant's figure and face through his mind. The applicant had a coy smile. A good lean body for a woman not young.

April studied the dreaming twinkle on Manny's face, pleased to see him happy.

"Another actor, you think?"

"No," replied Manny. "A writer of screenplays."

"One more of those? We should call this place Typewriters Anonymous."

Manny laughed.

April pushed. "Nothing to concern us about?"

Manny gave it some thought. "Maybe a little offbeat. Something about her, I don't know."

"Whoa," said April, waking up. "Two rentals in a year?"

"I spoke with her about that. She said she left the first place because of unbearable noise."

"And why the second place?"

"She said wants to be closer to Hollywood. She's been working here, and it takes too long a bus ride."

"That it does," said April.

They glanced at each other. How many more applicants to go through?

April wanted to believe. "She's not young, that's in her favor. And where does she live now?"

"With a friend, I think. Let me see it." He took the application from April. "She wrote down his number."

"Well, that's impressive. She has a friend." April smiled, resisting the urge to reject out of hand. She returned to the application. "Two apartments in Westwood, and in only one year, or less than that. She's from Queens. Interesting. Age, a guess?"

Manny rolled his eyes. "Forties, fifties."

"So, she works for, or did — a Maxwell Rupping?"

"Or Ripping? A private investigator," said Manny. "She seems a bright woman, I'll give her that."

And how he'd love to share her brightness, thought April. She took a deep breath in contemplation, studied Manny's hopeful expression.

He added, "She's got a good personality. No harm in checking out the app."

"You're right. We gotta make some calls on this one," said the 20-something manager, taking charge.

"Agreed, "said Manny, with pleasure. "Coffee?"

"Oh, no, thanks." April sprang to her feet. "I need to clean up my place, and I'm getting my hair done over this afternoon."

"Another make over so soon?"

April giggled like a bird born to giggle. She loved to giggle.

"That last so-called stylist saw me as Mae West. I don't want to be Mae West."

"You could do worse."

"Who next? Boy George?"

A shared laugh. April opened the door to leave.

Manny remembered: "Oh, that fellow up in 9, Cecil, was looking for you."

"Now what does he want?"

"Give him a chance, April."

"To do what, cast me in his new 1930s musical that nobody in this town is ever going to produce?"

"Since when did you want to be an actress?"

"I don't, but he thinks I should," she groaned. "Drink plenty of water, Manny." She smiled and left.

Manny relaxed in his cramped little studio, content to think of applicant Tiffany Orr, of how he and she might get to know each other were she to move in. At his advanced age, the Aussie transplant had willed himself to view older women as sex objects. Older, up to a certain age, certainly not that of Pearl Dubuque, in unit 7, with whom he enjoyed a relationship earning extra income as a make-believe on-call butler and all-around Man Friday. A long-forgotten second tier screen icon out of the 1920s, Dubuque, nonetheless, still carried on as if she, rather than her fantasied rival Gloria Swanson, was the real Norma Desmond. Except that for decades, Dubuque had dwelled not in a hillside mansion off Sunset Boulevard, but in the only two bedroom offered by Encore. Here, she was queen. Now and then she leaned out onto her balcony overlooking the street, as if to be looking for a runaway automobile belting up the driveway in escape mode, and, moments later, a handsome young man looking lost and stumbling up to the front door. That would be her cue to snare his attention and then to seduce him into her shut-off web of self-worship upstairs. She could see herself calling out over the balcony, "Hey, you down there!"

In vain, she spent a lot of time waiting for her dream runaway automobile to arrive. Walking out onto the balcony overlooking Springdale Way, to rehearse discovering its presence. Once getting carried away doing this, she was accused by a pedestrian passing by of undue solicitation. She scoffed him off, and went back inside.

Even in her wildest fantasies, only a couple miles away from Paramount Studios, Pearl Dubuque imagined the cameras rolling. And there would come a ring at the door, and she would peak through to see Manny standing outside — her stand-in Max von Mayerling. And he would bring her more fan letters just delivered.

After leaving Manny, April walked out through the front door of the building to sample the new day's swelter, a repeat of yesterday's, which had been a repeat of, it seemed, all the days before, stretching clear back to the Garden of Eden, California. Proud Angelinos, natives and all the rest from Ohio, all endured the torrid air as the price to pay for the gloriously warm mornings and evenings. Rarely, this year, had nights dipped below 70.

April walked up the driveway on the right side of the building to the parking area out back, to see if anything — or any stray bodies asleep — needed to be picked up or awakened, and to see how the garbage cans were holding out. Not yet full. She glanced over the parked cars lined up under the seven open roofed shelters. These slots were reserved for the one-bedroom renters. The studio tenants had to fend for themselves, parking their cars along the street.

Manny's stately old Buick, often mistaken for a studio prop when Manny had it out on the streets in motion, was parked in Pearl Dubuque's space. She had no car of her own, and so she had given the space to Manny, giving herself added leverage in extracting favors from him. In fact, she treated him like a part-time servant in the Max von Steinman mold – a role from the movie *Sunset Boulevard* that Manny played rather well, having more than once studied the film to improve upon the austerity of his imitation. He relied on the money Pearl Dubuque gave him, every so often, to make ends meet. Social Security was hardly enough for his low-budget version of Mayerling.

On rare occasions, the Great One (in her labored estimation) would summon Manny to chauffeur her around the area, the destination being another stop at the front gate to Paramount, just to wave hello to people who had no idea who she was, just to make an impression without suffering the rebuff of being refused admittance onto the lot. Manny, playing the stiff Mayerling to script, had to stifle his amusement. To survive in Hollywood without being hauled off in white to a nut house, one had to patronize the illusions of others.

After finishing her cursory inspection of the backyard, April went back inside, there to find another stiff character, Cecil Fanton, a Northern Californian transplant who had moved into Encore the year before. He was coming out of the laundry room. His face swelled into a grasping smile as wide as that of a circus clown. Fanton had fallen for April's old Hollywood visage, even finding her plumpish anatomy a visual virtue. She reminded him a little of Jean Harlow. He did not know whether to tell her, fearing that, were she on a diet, the intended flattery might sting.

Cecil Fanton was the "stage name" freely assigned to Herbert Clyde by an aging Hollywood press agent of yore, at present and likely forever withering away in the apartment building on Ivar where Cecil had lived just after coming to LA. Fanton had hit town hoofing with a built in Dick Powell shine. He was like a dancing Busby Berkeley bubble, ready to "revive" the grand old traditions of the 1930s movie musical. And how? Cecil had on his person folders of tunes and script ideas he had composed for the campaign, all of them pulsing to a style of pop music that had kept dance floors aswirl from the Great Depression through the Swinging Forties. In April Downing, Cecil saw the dawning face of a great new depression-era musical.

"Good morning, April!" he nearly sang.

"Good morning, Cecil," replied the flattered manager trainee.

"Sounds like a song I should write," said he, goaded on by the obligatory smile she flashed his way. "Good morning, April!"

"Oh, I like that," she sang, scattering a tease of giggles.

Cecil caught them like a grasping fan, feigning a shy school boy crush. Everything he did had the look of affectation. Inside, he felt a breakthrough. Surely she would not turn down the audition he would soon be offering her.

"First draft, April."

"I'm waiting for the final draft!" chirped April, gliding past Cecil while wondering why she had encouraged him as she did. What was I thinking? He does have a certain withered charm bordering on the antique, she reasoned.

And then she reasoned further: He really isn't all that bad looking. Not overweight. But that token mustache must go. *Adolf.* Who *else* was there on her scorecard? Of course Jerry, if only he were a little more ... not so normal. Would he still be working at the Glendale bakery for the rest of his life? The sweet fringe benefits on her table, were they to continue, would turn her still-manageable figure into a sky mate for the Good Year blimp.

Back inside, and ignoring the pink box, April felt an unprofessional urge to make calls to some of the references on Tiffany Orr's application. Sunday was not the best day for doing this. Many people would be going into churches. Or coming out of hangovers.

She wanted to call Ms. Orr's most recent manager, in Westwood. Alex had handed her total charge on this rental. Wait an hour or so, she instructed herself, and then call. She felt like a manager. And she took a break from her duties, glancing into the pink box, thinking, just one more glazed old fashion.

To compensate, she could always take a day off from Pink's hotdogs up the street.

# CHAPTER 2

Tiffany Orr charmed her way through a circular life. Sunday insulted her. Sunday was the day when people went to church, and church was one of the institutions she held in dubious regard. She hated anything that smacked of convention. Even the word itself — CONVENTION — drove her around the bend. In and around too much of it, she could feel herself slipping into an early coffin. And now, finding her post-hippie spirit cradled in the land of cardboard rainbows, she shimmered to the novel idea of dwelling in a place that still worshiped old fashioned lipstick. So old hat as to feel not conventional any more. But rather nouveau. She enjoyed mocking old social norms by painting up her lips in burgundy red and frosting off her head under a pink mini-umbrella hat. She would be ogled over by shallow aspiring actors, ogled over by tourists mistaking her for new Hollywood chic. She would stop them dead in their tracks — who *is* that woman?

A Queens, New York, native is who that woman is. One thing was certain about Ms. Orr from Queens. She relished life, or relished making herself and others believe that she did. Her modest, barely breasty figure was winsome, her face lush with luminosity. She caught the eye of men and then resented their advances. In Gotham East, she had been married for a number of listless years to a failed musician who taught high school for a living and had serial affairs with the sort of females, unlike Tiffany, who did not let tarot card readings dictate or challenge their every little move or mood.

Tiffany actually welcomed her husband's infidelities; for they freed her from a feeling of spousal obligation in the bed they technically shared. She could concentrate on her writing, such as it was, and on being hip and cool in the ambiguous Village scene, where she could share her disdain for the old-fashioned male animal with other like-minded feminists.

Running away always felt more alive than sticking to. Now she was running away, and at the same time running in circles back, in the most roundabout fashion, to her special "poet friend." This was the cowardly euphemism she used for a 27-year-old man who had a hard time holding down jobs, and who managed to survive on the streets, named Troy. The one thing he had little difficulty selling were his smoldering looks.

The two had met in a Village workshop for poets. The two had bonded easily, the glue being Tiffany's immediate attraction to his body and the praise she had showered upon the young poet's verse, some of which may have been valid. Troy was soon visiting Tiffany in her tiny Village studio, nudged in on the second floor of a corner building, with a direct view out onto blaring traffic. They shared a relish for the noise of New York City. Decades separating their ages, still they drew closer. Whenever Troy could see some sort of a payoff, cash or a space to crash, he warmed up to the next person wishing to befriend him. With Tiffany Orr, he could see a cool place to live, for a while at least, until he got another job and enough money to find an affordable space somewhere in Manhattan or Brooklyn.

And so he moved in. And so, Tiffany felt emboldened to move in on him, in her own slow, sly fashion. She now had the upper hand, but he still held out, and then gradually gave in as she wore down his resistance. One night, with more than a little help from wine, they had drawn carnally closer, and were nearing the point of no return when Troy all of a sudden turned aberrantly aggressive, but unable to perform conventionally, and tried switching the point of entry, which she resisted. He became violent in his desperate determination, and she had to fight him off her body. The whole charade they had been carrying on blew up in seconds.

In the traumatic wake of the botched encounter, he moved out. He knew he would not be welcomed back. But in time, they were talking again. Meeting at coffee houses, discussing poetry, sometimes taking in a flick. He harbored the hope that she would invite him back. She was close to asking him, but then, one night while walking down a busy Village street, in the window of a small café, Tiffany spotted Troy seated at a table with another woman, about Tiffany's age or older. The two appeared to be feasting on each other. Hoping not to be seen, Tiffany hurried on past, feeling used, inconsequential. She would get even. No way is he coming back into my life. Certainly, not into my bed!

A few days later, a call from her friend Steve, who lived in LA, gave her another idea. Steve had been after Tiffany to spend a week or so in California, to see if she might like living there. Actually, Steve wanted to get her away from a young man named Tom, really Troy, but Tiffany had kept the details of their affair self-servingly sketchy when she confided in Steve the trauma of that violent night with "Tom." Steve was now urging her once more to consider coming to Los Angeles, for a week or two. She could stay with him. Prone to rash moves on the spur of the moment, Tiffany gave up her apartment in the Village and made the move out to the city of angels.

Seated restlessly on a Greyhound "through bus" bound for Los Angeles, Troy was also on the run. He had managed to find Tiffany's Los Angeles address. But by the time the letter he had sent, hoping to start a reconciliation, had reached Westwood, Tiffany was no longer living there when it arrived. The letter was forwarded to Tiffany's next address, reaching it too late, as well. She was now living in a Hollywood Hotel, and hoping that Encore Apartments or one of the two other places to which she had applied would accept her.

She was running. Troy was running. Running to find each other somewhere in Los Angeles. At a poet's workshop. A vegetarian deli. On a street corner. Somewhere. He had to make amends, had to prove himself to himself — still. He knew that he could do it. Once in LA, he would go out to Tiffany's old address in Westwood, make inquiries. Someone would know.

April dialed the number for the manager of Tiffany's most recent address in Westwood.

"This is Verla," answered a. woman, who spoke in a lazy drawl.

"Hi, Verla. My name is April. I'm the on-site manager for Encore Apartments in Hollywood."

"Encore Apartments, the famous?"

"Yes," said April, giggling. "I'm so sorry to be calling on a Sunday."

"Oh, hell, hon, don't be sorry. Just be alive! Any day is okay with me. I have nothing else to do but entertain the famous Encore apartments."

"Oh, thank you, ah..."

"Verla, dear."

"Verla dear."

"That'll do, honey! And I think I know the reason for your charming call. Might one of our past renters be moving up in the world?"

"To Hollywood?"

Laughter.

"So, give me a name," said Verla, "and let's hope the spinning wheel doesn't get stuck on Trouble."

"Her name is Tiffany Orr."

"Oh, that one."

"Trouble?"

"Not exactly, no. So what does the wheel say?"

She looked amused. "How about Whirly bird!!"

April laughed. "Not too good?"

"One of those free spirits. Yes, she was here, not very long. We don't ask for a lease. Too many get broken. I don't like dealing with lawyers. And if I have to evict, nobody can do it faster than me."

"It sounds like I could learn a lot from you."

"Well, you have my number."

"I'll keep it, thank you!"

"Feel free," said Verla. "What can I say. Tiffany Orr, she's a charmer. A little, what, scatterbrained. Paid her rent on time. Anybody here who pays their rent on time deserves a few brownie points, no matter how else they carry on."

"And how else did she carry on?"

"Oh, let me think," answered Verla. "Single woman that age all come with baggage. She had a younger friend. I was not too impressed, from what I saw, but you can't judge. Anybody under twenty-five in this town is suspect."

April giggled, wondering if Verla was holding something back.

"I think she was hoping he would move in, and I told her she'd need to have him fill out another application. Nothing came of it. Is she applying for herself?"

"Yes, "said April.

"I guess she's alright, hon. But she didn't last long."

"Not even six months?"

"I think it was shorter than that. She wanted to be closer to Hollywood. She's writing the next great American novel. Likes people, I know that. She invited me to go with her to our locally famous Good Earth restaurant. She's one of those vegetarians. Me. I'm a burger and fries broad, ha! I hope this helps, April."

"It does. Thanks, it was fun talking to you."

"And you too," said Westwood to Hollywood. "Good luck, hon! Call me anytime. But wait for a couple of weeks. My man and I are going to Oklahoma to visit his brother."

"Well, do have fun."

"I'll try."

"Thank you!"

April rang off.

What to do with Ms. Orr, April wondered. Younger man. One of those. She laid the application out, and focused on a previous employer, picked up the phone and dialed his number. After only two rings, came a grim recorded voice: "You've reached VPI, Raymond Axton, very private investigator. Leave a message. I check these periodically."

The beep sounded.

April gave her name, position and phone number, and also Manny's number as a backup and asked for a reference on Tiffany Orr.

After hanging up, she felt productive. And a little more professional by digging deeper into the applicant's background.

Time for a break, and there it was, all in pink and waiting to be ravished. Please, take a little more of me!, she could almost hear the box pleading. April snarled back, get lost! She struck the lid shut, picked it up, intent on taking it down to the laundry room where others could have at it. She got halfway down the hall, and then, sudden guilt crushed her spirit. What she was about to do would be tantamount to giving away any gift that Jerry might give her in the future? How ungrateful. She reversed course and walked back, and placed the box of day-old pastries back on the table, and felt much better. Then she went across the hall to see if Manny was in.

On Sunday afternoon the same day, Troy, sitting bored stiff on the "through bus," the sort that always goes through every single town off the road, no matter its size, was brooding, still, over the horrible night at Tiffany's that got him kicked out. How she had made him feel desired, only to deny him his preferred mode of expressing himself. Hell, a lot of men preferred the same thing. Now he felt a terrible pit of defeat and guilt in his stomach. She had left him like feeling like a bumbling lover. Loser, loser. But, it was not the first time he had failed with a woman.

Out the window, more of the same boring brown. Endless. Empty. How drab a life for any fool who puts up with all that brown! He should write a poem about it. Would it ever end? The dull listless color entrapped his soul, and he suddenly felt like getting off the bus at the next stop and returning to New York. Except, he didn't have the money in his pocket to afford the fare.

He looked across the aisle to a young fellow half asleep. He should have been social when the guy tried talking to him at the soda machine during a rest stop back there. It might have been worth his while, a little friendship, and possibly more in the bank. Westwood. Where the hell is Westwood, he wondered. He knew that's where she lived. It sounded like a village in the Hamptons. He should have been social with the guy across the aisle. Maybe when he wakes up.

On the same Sunday afternoon in Los Angeles, April was listening to Manny's phone across the hall not being answered. He had still not returned.

And then, April's own telephone rang out.

She took the call. "Hello?"

"Hi, ah, this is Tiffany Orr."

"Oh yes," answered April, warming to the voice.

"And you are April?"

"Yes, I am."

"I was by yesterday, and I'm very sorry if I'm calling you at the wrong time. Mr. Sheffield gave me your number to call."

"Not a problem. We have it before us, Ms. Orr. We are processing it."

"Good news," chirped the caller. "I am being processed!"

"Yes, you are!"

"But not, I hope, into processed cheese, please," said Tiffany effervescently.

They laughed.

"I was wondering, I just happen to be in the area, and I could drop by."

April, already charmed, was keenly interested in the woman "Yes, do come by. My unit is the first you see to your left, on the ground floor."

"Great! I think I'm only a few blocks away. Maybe five minutes?"

"Take as many as you need."

"Thanks, April."

"You're very welcome, Ms. Orr. See you."

April rang off. Now, that was fun, she thought, looking forward to meeting the applicant face to face. She could imagine this woman bringing a nice breezy personality to a unit upstairs that had suffered the gloom and destruction of its two previous tenants. Not quite yet, said her new managerial voice within: Dig deeper into this one.

The bell on April's door sounded about ten minutes later. And when she opened it, there stood a vibrant woman brimming with life on a lovely face that had aged well. Of a figure slender and compact. Of blondish hair that swirled above her head like a retro 1930s hat piece.

"You are April," Tiffany sang.

"Yes," I am. "And you are Tiffany?"

"I am!"

Please, come in."

Tiffany entered April's cheerful space, the walls adorned with fanciful child-like paintings, the work of a previous boyfriend of April's who refused to grow up, and with some celebrity photographs. In the kitchen sink, stacks of dirty dishes had piled up.

"I love the building," said Tiffany.

"It's a gem, isn't it," agreed April. "Please, sit down, maybe at the table. We can talk for a bit." The messy sink prodded April. "Sorry for the mess. These are not business hours."

"And I'm charmed over your allowing me the visit."

"Think nothing of it. Something to drink? Tea, coffee, water?"

Tiffany mulled it over.

"Diet water?" suggested April.

Tiffany laughed. "Plain water would be fine."

April brought Tiffany a glass of water, settled into her chair, and turned a little more serious. She had better, she thought.

"So, please tell me, Tiffany, "she started, "What made you want to leave lovely Westwood?"

Tiffany let go of a heavy sigh. "Westwood."

April giggled. "Yes, it can become a little too much of itself out there. Nice and pretty, and pretty dull."

"But I love this area," oozed Tiffany.

"Isn't it a charm," agreed April, wishing she could give wing to Ms. Orr's application right now and be done with the tedious process. Run it past Alex, first, that other voice inside her was yelling.

"So, Manny said you like the unit."

"It's perfect!" sang Tiffany Orr. "I travel lightly, and I like the peaceful atmosphere down here. I write screenplays — on the side. Still struggling."

April smiled. There were so many people in this town who wrote screenplays on the side, that she deemed it about equal to watching TV on the side.

"It's nice and quiet up there on the second floor," April began, and why did I say quiet, she rued. "Nobody above you. Did Manny tell you the studios do not come with parking?"

"No problem," smiled Tiffany. "I don't come with a car." And, as if proud of the fact, "Nothing to park."

"Perfect," said April. "And, did he tell you, no pets?"

"He did. The only pet I have is a stuffed bunny I found on the street. It looked so sad."

"How touching!" said April, wondering, provisionally unimpressed, if Ms. Orr was an animal rights do-gooder.

The phone rang. April took the call, but before she could barely say hello, Manny's hushed voice interrupted her. "Shhh! Manny here. Don't let on."

April immediately feigned talking to somebody else. "Yes, and how are you?"

Manny hushed, "Is Ms. Orr in there with you7"

"Oh, no, I haven't forgotten. Are we still on for today?"

Manny whispered, "Don't say yes, not yet. Her boss left a message on my machine. Sounds on the fence to me."

April said, "Oh, sure. This afternoon sounds fine, Maureen. I'll meet you there."

She placed the telephone back in its cradle, and turned to Tiffany.

"A friend. We're meeting for lunch."

"Oh, then I better be going," said Tiffany, springing to her feet, glad that April had not raised the subject of the deposit required, afraid of what it might be. Cross that bridge if I get there.

"I've enjoyed meeting you, Ms. Tiffany Orr."

Why did she put it that way, Tiffany wondered, sensing an ominous shift in April's tone.

April accompanied Tiffany to the door, and opened it for her. "So, we will run your application past the owner, he's out of town for a day or so, and, say, get back to you in two or three days, at the most?"

"Wonderful," said Ms. Orr.

"Great meeting you Tiffany. In touch soon!"

"Okay, thanks!"

Tiffany exited down the hall, and out onto the sidewalk, and glanced up the street. He was there, as promised, parked up on the next block, waiting for her.

April waited for a few moments, and then hurried across the hall to Manny's apartment, knocked on the door. He let her in. The two sat down at the small round table, and listened to the message left by Raymond Axton on Manny's old phone mate machine for a Tiffany Tarter. "Been here on and off, what, two or three months ... one of those free spirit types, pretty reliable, I suppose, considering I only give her part time work, although at the moment, she's more or less full time. There was one incident, a friend who dropped by. Or did it involve? No, that was somebody else, I think. Yes. She's okay."

The message ended.

Manny looked at April: "What do you think?"

"Tiffany Tarter? As in tartar sauce?"

"That's what it sounds like to me. So, anyway, I called up Mr. Axton. He was there. I described our Orr, and he said it matched his Tarter, bone for bone."

April giggled. "What did you give him, Manny, an x-ray printout?"

Manny cracked a sunny smile. "I tried to dig deeper, for it sounded like he might be protecting her."

April shrugged. "From what?"

"I asked him that," answered Manny, popping a suspicions face. "He pulled back, said he had confused our applicant for somebody else."

"Oh, really. So, what are you thinking?"

Manny forced his rational nature to trump his infatuation with the applicant. "So, she's a free spirt, and she moves around a lot. Two rentals in a year. Did you reach the apartment house manager in Westwood?"

"Yes, she thinks Orr is alright. Had a lot of younger friends."

"Male?"

"Yes."

Manny plotted. "So ... maybe we should go out there and ask around, talk to some of the renters coming or going. They're the ones who spill the beans."

"That's an idea. But I've already spoken with the manager."

"Then me?"

"Oh, wait. She said she was leaving early Monday morning on vacation."

April was now picturing a long leisurely ride out Sunset Boulevard in Manny's ostentatious old motor machine.

"Yes, Manny. Let's do that!"

"I'll polish up the car."
"We're not parading?"
"Why not?"

April grinned joyfully. She loved riding around with Manny in the old Buick with the top down, being seen by tourists who might mistake them for Hollywood somebodies.

Manny's charm gave her life a buoyancy. She had her parents in Burbank to fall back upon whenever she needed to, and she had Manny, every day at Encore.

# CHAPTER 3

Monday dawned perfectly composed — an exact imitation of the perfect Sunday preceding it. Tiffany felt a rise walking down South Sycamore towards Steve's one bedroom, just above Melrose. They had spoken by phone the night before, and Tiffany had said she would be dropping by about now. She hated coming by when he unexpectedly had company, usually his latest boyfriend or maybe a "trick" he'd brought home. Had Steven not been so promiscuous, Tiffany might have accepted his offer to stay a few nights at his place while in-between apartments. She relished the idea, for it might draw them closer. Anything to get physically closer to the non-straight Steven.

The two had known each other since their teen years, growing up on the same block in Queens. Tiffany had harbored a long and lingering crush on Steven's good, if average looks, on his solid build and outgoing personality, and she envied all of the men he routinely met at the bars. Only weeks before Steven's moving to Los Angeles, two years ago, did he finally come out to her. By then, she had suspected, and so she transitioned into confidante. They remained friends, in some ways better friends than before. They could cry on each other's shoulder. But Troy was a name

Steven did not know. Tom was the name Tiffany used for Troy, whenever talking about him to Steven.

Tiffany lived vicariously through Steven's gay conquests, wishing she could be one of them. Waiting for a chance, somehow, someway, to lure him closer with her womanly wiles. She would issue flirtatious hints, and he would receive them as harmless flattery, none too bothered by the attention. She was yet to offer Steve a foot massage, she was still waiting for the right moment. This was one of her most effective ways to break down a man's resistance. Feet first, then fingers north.

She was knocking on Steve's door, as was the plan they agreed to the previous day during a telephone call, but he was not answering. Had he forgotten? Had she come too late? She remembered mentioning nine o'clock. From here, after a brief visit, she would continue on to her job at the Axton agency. It was now a few minutes after nine. Might he still be in there, asleep? He had Monday's off from his job managing a copy shop. She assumed this would be the best time to come by without having to share him with some stranger he had just picked up. She pushed the bell once more. She was planning to ask him for a possible loan were she to need the help on a deposit for the apartment.

Steve's place was on the ground floor of a 10-unit building of one bedrooms, wrapped in a lush botanical spectacle of free-flowing flowers, each unit with its own patio or balcony, each dressed in abundant foliage Postcard LA. The building stood on the west side of South Sycamore in a leafy neighborhood, half a block north of Melrose, and only a block east of La Brea, where the famous Pinks Hot Dog grill stood.

And there he was, just as Tiffany was turning away to leave, hobbling up the walk with a strange fellow, both of them tipsy, the fellow leaning heavily upon Steve's broad shoulders.

"Tiffany!" sang her inebriated friend. "Oh, Tiffy, I was supposed to be here . Hope I'm not too late."

No, Steve."

"We rushed back, didn't we ... Mack? Mark?"

The soused visitor looked confused.

"Either," he slurred.

Now who has he brought home, Tiffany wondered with a sinking pause. He had been bringing all sorts of men into his apartment since having split up with Gary. Gary's sudden desertion had been a crushing blow. The two had been "dating" for almost a year, seeming to be coming closer to moving in together and declaring themselves a couple. But Gary had grown weary of Steven's overly romantic attachment, unable to commit to the monogamy that Steven was holding out for.

"Tiffany, just in time. Meet my new friend, ah ... ah, Mark, right?"

"Mack," said Steve's new friend. "Hello." He was hardly looking at her.

"Say hello, Tiffany, to Mark. I mean... ah..."

Mack thought a little. "Mark is alright, Tiffany."

Tiffany forced a laugh, thoroughly put off by the stumbling reception she was getting from her best friend. He must have forgotten. He was drunk. She hated him drunk. She blamed it on the split with Gary, which he was still trying to get over. Another careless tryst, she thought, to help salve the pain. She hated to see him constantly on the prowl.

"We are just coming back from – where were we, Mark. Right, *Mark*?"

"Now I'm not sure myself."

"From... where are we coming from, Mack?"

"Breakfast. Remember? Next to the bar where you met me."

"And what was the bar?"

"I can't remember. I'd never been there before."

Tiffany smiled wanly, wanting to get through this insulting reception as soon as possible.

"You are coming in, aren't you, Tiffany?"

"Oh, I just came by, Steven, to see if there were any messages for me. I've applied at a few apartments."

"Sure you have, sure! That's right. You called yesterday. And we talked, right? Oh jeez, and I forgot all about it, Tiffany. I owe you!"

"That's okay, Steve. I do have to run, up to my job."

"Your job, sure, Tiff. I'll go in and look, I will I will! You wait there, Mack, and keep my best friend happy."

"Hello, his best friend," slurred Mack or Mark with a woozy smile.

Steven went inside. Mack straightened up and smiled dumbly at Steven's best friend, wondering if she might be competition.

"Looks like a sunny day," said Tiffany trying to be civil, But fuming inside.

"It does look sunny, it does," mumbled Mack or Mike, squinting up at the sky.

"And where's your job?"

"Up on Hollywood, near Western."

"Oh yes, one of my favorite bars—clubs is up there."

Steven returned.

"Red light was on," he announced. "No messages for either of us."

Tiffany's spirit sunk. "Nothing."

"Come on in for a moment, Tiff!"

"Oh, I can't Steve. I'm already late for work."

"You always are," he grinned. "Don't break your record."

"I'll call you later, Steve."

"Yes, do!"

She glanced at Mack or Mike. "Nice meeting you."

"I think so," he mumbled, leaning towards Steven.

Steve waved. "Bye!"

"Bye," echoed the other man.

Tiffany gave a half-wave, and hurried off, wanting to flush the scene from her mind, wanting to think better of Steve. How she wished she had met Gary. Steven had talked about him with such poignancy, as if Gary had been — or would have been — the love of his life. They had made plans to travel to Europe together, and to take in museums and concerts. Gary had infected Steven with his love of music and art. She could see such change in her old Queens friend. And when the two broke up, she wanted to believe that they were destined to get back together. While Steve dried another steam of tears, she told him that, sometimes there were second chapters in love. She had a way of lifting the spirits of others, her most authentic attribute. If only she could lift her own — onto a more normal path, and maybe find what Steven had almost found with Gary.

Now, hastening off from the scene of another likely one-night stand, she felt relieved that she had not moved in with Steven. He took too many foolish chances, in her view, bringing men home after having met them only hours before, or minutes. Too many chances. Thank God she had not. Thank God for the rundown Stargazer motel on Sunset, where she was now staying. At least, there she had control. Privacy. How prudent and glad she felt, not sleeping in there on Steve's couch and being awakened at any hour by his hauling in another one. Who knows when he might host the next hillside strangler?

A little later on Monday morning, April was gazing out her kitchen window up onto a pure baby blue sky, and hearing the rumble of Manny's old Buick slowly backing out of its space and then up the driveway. The car's rusty honk went off, her cue that he was out there at the wheel, waiting. She left her apartment in a flourish, as if she were embarking on a trip abroad, and scampered down the front steps, onto the sidewalk. Standing above it all, perched over the edge of her balcony behind a pair of enormous sun glasses, towered, if a little wobbly, Pearl Dubuque, wondering what the two were up to.

Manny pulled slowly away from the curb, hoping to impress and make jealous the eyes of his benefactor above.

"Is she up there looking down?"

April craned her neck.

"She's out on the balcony! You're on, Manny!"

Manny cracked a big smug smile.

"You are such a cad!"

"Won't hurt her knowing I have other prospects."

April showered a flock of giggles into the warm air.

Manny motored up to Hollywood and Vine, so that they could cruise west on Hollywood, past the hordes of out-of-towners who would gawk at the sight of them. April enjoyed the attention. Her Clara Bow look suited the antiquity of the car. The flattered Manny found it all very amusing.

Crossing La Brea going west, the crowds faded away, and Manny let his stagey airs down, and looked over at April.

"So, the baker boy is not Mr. Right?"

"Oh, I don't know," she answered. "We've only known each other, what, three or four weeks?"

"In this town, that's a future."

April understood his theme. "So, the reason you like Jerry is because he has a regular job and we get all those leftover donuts?"

"No, no," Manny countered. "Because he *has* a job."

April groaned. She knew he was right. She relaxed as they rolled through a more prosperous section of new high-rise apartments that felt miles away from the gaudy glitz and the excited crowds at Grauman's Chinese Theatre.

"How different it is, today," he said. "Nobody can commit. Maybe I was lucky."

"I know," said April. "Your wife."

"Oh, what a pal she was."

Here comes another testimonial to the love of his life, thought April. But she would never make light of it. She liked hearing Manny say the same old things, because, his undying love for his late wife gave April reason to believe that she could find the same thing, were she ever so lucky.

"Oh, what a pal she was. Could put me to sleep, pat me a little, and I'd purr like a kitten."

He'd purr like a kitten. One of April's favorite lines. Purr like a kitten. In a way, he still was purring, and she envied what he had known. And she was happy for him.

Manny steered his imperial-feeling Buick into a left turn on Fairfax, it purred and sputtered down to Sunset, where he routed it west. Soon, the scenery turned perfectly green and blossomed almost larger than life as they entered the tranquil world of Beverly Hills. Every bush and shrub looked artfully pruned and shaped. Joggers in tight flashy latex streaked by. The farther west they went, the larger became the homes on reclusive hillside estates, each nestled, half hidden, amidst resting trees. Westwood, now presently ahead, bloomed with its lovely homes and handsome apartment buildings, occupied by professors and research scientists and smart young students. Only blocks away was the woodsy terrain of UCLA.

"Oh, what a place to live," sighed April, imagining what it might be like living in a dreamy hillside house with a dreamy husband, raising a dreamy family.

Manny slowed down. "There it is — Hilgard." He turned left onto the street, and cruised slowly down it. "We're looking for?"

April had a slip of paper in hand. "947."

"Not far."

Apartment buildings to the right, family homes to the left, and all of them covered with enough blossoms to stock a complete Rose Parade.

"There it is!" said April.

"And what luck," added Manny. "An apartment for rent."

They saw a distinguished two-story building of high end red brick, the grass and bushes out front well-tended to. Manny decided it would be best for April to inquire. He found a parking space up the street, where he would wait for her.

She got out in a gust of giggles, and walked back up the street, to the address. As she approached the front door, it opened and a young woman barely more than a girl stepped half way out, to sniff the air, and to look about.

"Good morning," said April, cheerfully.

"Good morning," answered the girl, not as cheerfully.

"I see you're renting."

"Two units. But the manager's away, and her assistant won't be back until this afternoon."

"Oh, that's a bummer," said April, smiling. "I'm April."

"I'm Jane," said the other. "You're looking?"

"I love this neighborhood. I've been wanting to make a move. This building looks so settled."

"Settled? Sometimes, I suppose."

"Not always?"

"Well, they just got rid of two problems."

"Oh, really?" said April, careful not to press.

"At least they evict people here in short order."

"So ... what happened?"

"Oh, drugs, the usual. One of the renters, older woman, had a young guy in there living with her, we think. They got her out fast."

"Really?"

"Bad news, but I liked her. And now, I can't remember her name. They come and go so fast. I think she gave foot massages. Verla, the manager, she's back in Oklahoma right now, she could tell you a lot."

"Verla?"

"Yes." The woman laughed. "I think she tried putting the make on one of the woman's friends."

"Really?"

"It got messy. They accused her of solicitation, ha! That's like accusing somebody here of breathing! But they got her out in a hurry."

"Oh, goodness," said April, "well, I'm impressed with management."

"Riff raff doesn't riff around here for very long here, and that's just fine with me — as long as it's not *my* riff raff!"

April sprayed a chorus of giggles across the lawn, as she turned to leave. "Nice talking to you!"

"Come back later, April," said Jane, pleased with her humor. "Margaret, the assistant, should be here then."

"I might, Jane!"

On April's way back down to the sidewalk, a strange surprise came walking in her direction. He looked familiar—the man she had seen standing on the driveway between Encore Apartments and the white building? He passed her, looking away, and she turned to watch him going up the path to the front door and letting himself in.

She walked back to Manny's car, got in, and they drove off.

"Got anything?" he asked.

"Plenty."

"So, whenever you're ready, do make it good."

April was ready. She gave Manny a full account.

Manny looked intrigued to learn of the foot massages. Actually, it gave his sleeping hormones a reason to wake up. How nice it was, at his inactive age, to feel stirred. And without pills.

The next morning, Tuesday, Tiffany was dialing Steven's number, hoping to catch him at home, as sometimes he had Tuesday off as well as Monday.

"Yeah, Steven here."

"You sound at the end of a work shift, Steve."

"Oh, and what shift it was, Tiff. Such wonderful work. And in my own home. I took the day off, called in sick. I am sick – for him! Heaven came back last night. Two nights going on three. Heaven, so far."

"He's there now?"

"No, no. He left already. Had to get up early for work, while I was sleeping. I was looking around, relieved. He's passed another post-exit inventory. TV's still here, although I rather wish somebody would take it, I need a kick to get a new one. Spare change by my bed untouched. My Sony Walkman on the shelf, still. Lust and trust in the same package. Now, that's a keeper. And what about you, Tiffany?"

"You are very funny, Steve. About me? Boss doesn't need me today. I was thinking you might like to meet for brunch, somewhere ..."

"Sounds perfect. Just not the Good Earth, please."

"No, it's your turn, you pick!"

Steve thought. "How about the bad earth? What say I meet you up at Pancakery in Silverlake? About an hour."

"Yes!"

"An hour it is."

# CHAPTER 4

Tuesday morning found April on the second floor making her usual rounds, once again wishing that Wayne would emerge from Unit 10 on his way to work, and, best of all, be wearing the cut off she'd spotted him in the day before when he was going up the stairs. If only, a close-up. Ambling down the hall to stall for time, she heard a loud crashing sound from within. God, let it be him, she prayed. The door to Wayne's apartment flew open, and out stormed Melissa.

April, jolted, could not resist. "Good morning."

"Rotten morning," said Melissa, slamming the door shut, Storming down the hall, her face on fire.

"Everything alright?" called out April.

"Where the hell is he," said the would-be actress, vanishing down the staircase in flat angry stomps.

Cecil came out of his unit, looked around. He was wearing a cut off similar to what April had seen Wayne wearing, but Cecil's average body did nothing to flatter it. Fashion did not make *this* man. In fact, April decided that she preferred him in something Nelson Eddy might have worn.

"What was that all about?" he asked

April shrugged. "Who knows?"

Cecil grinned at April like a dog wanting to lick her. She was growing accustomed to his awkward shows of interest, and learning to feel flattered by them.

"Did you hear anything in there last night, Cecil?"

"No, come to think of it. Maybe they took the day off."

A telephone ring went off inside the unit. April and Cecil listened to it ring, over and over, until it stopped.

April shook her head. "I'm sorry about the situation in there. You are a good tenant, and deserve better. We are working on it, I can assure you."

"And that's good of you," said Cecil. "It's not all that bad, really. Just, well, sometimes a bit dramatic. She was friendly with me once, told me she goes out on auditions and sometimes rehearses scenes with Wayne."

"Yes," said April, unimpressed, "that's the line they give us. But they won't be here very long if they don't can it."

"She is a bit moody," he volunteered.

"A bit?"

"I wouldn't want to tangle with her."

"No, you wouldn't," agreed April, not about to reveal her own tangled designs on Melissa's boyfriend.

"But, now *you*," said Cecil, casting a leering Groucho Marx eye onto the woman who collected his rent. "Oops. You're the manager now. I better be good." He laughed self-servingly.

"Yes, you better," said April, feeling like she might throw up. "Have a nice Sunday, Cecil."

"Shall I turn that into a song? Guy has a crush. Girl sings, have a nice Sunday, with somebody else?" He was pleased with his cleverness.

April found Cecil Fanton's stagey self-regard amusing, and so she tossed him a few giggles, but went back down the hall, and down the stairs, and into her apartment, just as the phone was ringing. She took the call.

"Hello?"

"Encore apartments?" The caller had a lurching voice.

"It is."

"You left a message about a woman I once employed, Tiffany Orr, giving me as a reference."

"Oh, are you Mr. ...?"

"Maxwell Rupping."

"Well, yes, thanks."

"She worked for me, part time. Answering phones, typing up orders."

"What sort of a business are you in, Mr. Ripping?"

"Rupping. Not Ripping."

"Oh, sorry. I thought."

"They all do. I'm not a ripper. I'm a rupper."

Did he say "rubber, April wondered. She heard a high baritone guffaw. And probably a failed comedian, too, she guessed.

"You want to know what I do? Consultations."

April pushed on. "About?"

"Whatever the customer needs advice on."

"Oh, I see," said April, trying her best not to alienate the caller.

"She was here, on and off, over a month or two. Part time, so I can't fault her much, if she failed to show a couple of occasions. She was okay. A bit new age, all about hanging out with a younger crowd, that type, but they all are."

"So, why did she leave you, Mr. Rubber?"

"Not Rubber. Rupper."

"I am so sorry."

"Just call me Max."

"That's easy."

"Why did she leave? No idea. I never poke. Okay, that's about it."

"Thank you, ah, Max."

"You're Encore Apartments, right?"

"Yes."

"Oh that's in...."

"Hollywood."

"Sure. I've been there, Miracle Mile."

"Yes."

"Down on ..."

"Springdale Way."

"Have a good whatever," he snapped. "I'm rupping off," and his phone connection vanished.

April wondered, did he say he was rubbing off, or rupping off? She had to run across the hall to share this with Manny. Good at least for chuckles and coffee.

Seated outside, at a small sidewalk table in front of the Pancakery on Sunset, having a late morning breakfast under a warm blue late morning sky, Tiffany was facing a more receptive Steven. Well, she had him all to herself, that is, when he was not distracted by passing male figures up and down the street.

Steven was giving the eye to the circular sweep of Tiffany's large pink hat. "Pink's a good color on you," he said, picturing his latest trick in a pink tank top, and she wanted to believe he was sending her a hint. Wanted to believe that Steven was really "bi."

He spotted another object of interest, across the street. "And look who I see, over there in front of the Rusty Spike. It can't be?"

"Who?"

"An old flame. Please don't come over here."

"Not Gary?"

"No, but how I wished," answered Steven, who sank into a morose funk. "And are you psychic, Tiffany. Time for your tarot cards! I ran into somebody last night who knows Gary."

"You did?"

Steve beamed. "Seems that Gary and whoever he has been seeing broke up."

"Good news for you, Steve!"

"How I wish. How I wish."

"You haven't seen him much?"

"Not in, what, six or seven months. I think he stopped going to the bars we went to. I almost did, afraid to run into him."

"I'm sorry."

"I'm still getting over it. And now."

"Now what?"

"I'd like to find out more about his situation. The guy I talked to gave me a number to call, somebody close to Gary, I gave the guy my number. Maybe he'll pass it along to Gary."

"Well, I hope he does, for your sake."

Steve sighed in residual pain, and shifted the mood. "Anyway, another hopeless infatuation on the back burner. But what about you, Tiffany? Heard any more about your boyfriend back in New

York? The younger guy."

"Nothing," she answered, shrugging off the question.

"You're just as well off without him. Wasn't he the one who tried to strangle you?"

Tiffany shook all over. How blunt of Steve to be so insensitive! To hear the words spoken, it made the incident feel even more traumatizing.

"No, no,' she willfully lied. "That was somebody else, Steve."

"What was his name?"

"You mean, Tom?"

"The one who ..."

"Yes, Tom."

She had lied back in New York, to save face. In fact, she had never used the name Troy, in order to shield a shabby and dangerous liaison from Steve, in case the affair revived itself and she might have to introduce Troy to Steven.

"You do collect them, Tiff!" said Steve, making the wary face of a concerned friend. "I should talk."

Yes, he should, thought Tiffany, remaining tactfully silent on the matter, and feeling pleased with herself that she had not told Steve about Dexter, her new student friend from UCLA in Westwood.

But now it was Tiffany's turn to be startled by a figure across the street, standing idle and staring her way.

"What are you looking at, Tiff?"

"Somebody from ... Is that him, over there?"

Steve scanned the possibilities. "The man in the brown shirt?"

"Yes."

"Needy, but a little interesting," ventured Steve. "Maybe we could make a swap, my stalker for yours?"

They burst out laughing. Birds of the same precarious feather.

"You know him, Tiff?"

"I'm not sure. I may, from my last apartment."

"You want to leave?"

"Yes," said Tiffany. "Why don't we."

"Fine with me."

They called the waiter over, paid and left.

Tiffany was satisfied to be walking with Steve, and feeling so fulfilled. If only ... "So what are your plans for the afternoon,

Stevie?"

"I promised Mack, or ...?

"Mark."

"Okay, for today he's Mark. We might meet up when he gets off work around three, I hope."

Tiffany made up her mind. "I'm off to Westwood to visit Maureen."

"The Good Earth?"

"How'd you guess?"

"Hey, there's your bus!"

"Great timing!"

They ran. Steve hurried with Tiff up the bus stop, and she went aboard. "Call you later!"

"Okay!" Steve waved, and then went back up the block and into the Rusty Nail, intent on calling up Mack (or Mark), hoping the background noise of a bar would make him jealous. He was thinking of all the looks Tiffany had given him. In her own way, he had to admit, she cut an attractive figure. If only he could find her personality in a man.

After his Greyhound pulled into the Hollywood depot on Vine that Tuesday morning, Troy went to the payphone in the lobby, anxious to dial the Los Angeles number he had in hand for Tiffany. He had obtained it in Manhattan from a friend of Tiffany's. When he had dialed it a few weeks ago, after hearing Tiffany's voice greeting, he felt too insecure to leave a message before actually being in Los Angeles. Afraid that if she answered and he did not get the reception he hoped for, he would not make the trip at all.

Now, he was dialing the same number for the second time, ready to say something were she not in or did not pick up, ready to lay on his moody charm — his primary asset — to surprise her with his presence in this casually seductive city. To tell her how he hoped the change of scenery would pull him out of his creative funk.

The phone made a couple of rings. He waited for a message machine to activate.

"The number you have dialed has been disconnected. Please hang up, if you think you have dialed in error, and dial again."

He hung up in a fit, dialed again, and got that same superior

Ma Bell voice.

Pissed, he jammed the phone into its' cradle, walked up Vine, feeling like he had lost before having even being given a second chance. He had come all this way, for what? He only wrote poems when he was in a certain mood. In Tiffany's company, she had helped him believe in himself, had lavished praise on his work, even over verse she knew fell short of the mark. He had brought little with him, only a medium sized backpack crammed with pens and pads and sheets of paper upon which he had scribbled ideas; with clothes and magazines, a few basic toiletries, and a small book of Hart Crane poems.

Up Vine Street, he came upon an outdoor burger stand that looked like it belonged on a carnival midway. He took a stool and ordered eggs and bacon and fries and a coke.

He liked the hot sticky air. One for L.A.

Almost immediately, a pleasant middle-aged man sat down on the stool next to his. Moments passed. The man next to Troy said something that Troy hardly heard, he was too engrossed in his own confusion, trying to figure out what to do next. He only knew that Tiffany was living in a place called Westwood. He only knew, and what a lifeline it felt like now, that he had her Westwood address with him. He had managed to extract it from the woman in the Village who had rented the room to Tiffany.

The man next to him was going on about the Dodgers. Was he talking to Troy? He could only have been talking to Troy, for there was nobody on the other stool next to the fellow. Troy knew the type. He had been given looks by many people across gender lines. Troy decided it might be to his advantage to listen. He was all alone in a strange place known for its heartless addiction to youth and sex. He had those things. So, if he could not find Tiffany, why not give it a try anyway?

"Their pitchers stink," moaned the dull fellow sitting to his left.

"You think so?" said Troy. He listened to the man ranting on about a baseball team that he, Troy, a Yankees fan, cared little for.

"Oh, my name's Tyler," said the man reaching out to shake the hand of the stunning young find directly to his right

"Troy."

By the time Tiffany arrived in Westwood, she had decided that, rather than Maureen, she would first try Dexter, calling him from a payphone, on the spur. She was at her best on the spur. Dexter was in when she called, and he sounded excited to hear her voice, and readily agreed to meet at the Good Earth in about a half hour. They had only known each other less than a month, having first met outside the theatre at the Los Angeles County Art Museum, the night a John Ford film was being screened. He, too, wanted to write screenplays, and so they had exchanged numbers and, a couple of weeks later, were facing each other at the Good Earth. Dexter was a student at UCLA, majoring in film studies.

Tiffany had a date. She felt a bounce to the new day. The morning sun was casting a sleepy glow over the well-scrubbed streets, glistening under a radiant sheen of drying mist. To kill time, she ambled down Broxton, looked at the displays in store windows, walked down to the corner to enjoy the young crowd, and then back up to the restaurant. She went inside and secured a table for two against the wall, and sat down. And dreamed. Dexter might do. Twenty years younger, stretching it. Well, not thirty or forty years. True. And if people give us those disapproving looks, let them! What do I have to be ashamed of? In fact, she was drawn to the challenge of trying to seduce gay and bi-sexual men, in whose company she did not feel threatened, as she did with straight men. Nor did she feel out of place taking the lead. Being in control.

Steve wondered if she were a closet lesbian, and when he put the question to her, she made the most ghastly face. "Yikes!"

And the two laughed, but he still wondered.

## CHAPTER 5

Troy was walking down Vine Street towards Sunset, feeling more stable and even anchored, because he had in his pocket a phone number for the Dodger fan who had befriended him at the carny grill. On Sunset, he would take a bus to Westwood. And out there, wherever the place was, maybe he would find her.

His best chance for a start was at the address he had for the apartment Tiffany had rented when she first came to Los Angeles, before moving into the other apartment on Hilgard. About a half hour on the bus, and most of the riders were gone. He was gazing out the window at the gleaming elegance of vegetation-lush Beverly Hills, feeling glad that he had come west, even were he never to find Tiffany. Glad, because the abundance of sunshine lifted his spirit. He sometimes wondered if he'd been born to a frown on his mother's face.

The people who rode the bus had behaved remarkably well; a far cry from straightahead, stay-out-of-my-face New Yorkers. And how small a place LA, up close, appeared to be, so far. A peaceful succession of rather plain little towns spreading endlessly in every which direction, on and on and on. He was comparing it favorably to New York and all of New York's smug self-proclaimed genius poets and writers, and all of the whoring agents back there jumping over each other to sign the latest Fitzgerald.

He'd read one of his poems in a Village coffee house; and the response was mute. Afterwards, the few who approached him with fawning flattery turned out to be more interested in sampling his body than his body of work. But then, when Tiffany Orr joined the circle of early adulation, she came across more like a friend wanting to share. She herself was one of the many nobodies, and to that Troy could relate. But was her praise to be believed? In truth, Tiffany Orr doled it out generously, hoping to receive the same in return. She ignored Troy's crude outpourings, dwelled instead on the raw flashes of talent she saw in his writing, this to bolster his frail ego. Let the envious poets and pompous teacher-critics take his work apart. She would give him the supporting friendship he needed to put his work and himself back together.

Troy could feel his New York grudges melting away under the bright sunny sky, and he could see why so many people were drawn to the weather. He got off the bus near the Westwood Village shopping district, knowing he was close to his destination, and wanting, first, to spend some time walking through the bustling throngs of attractive young people everywhere. So many faces and figures to enjoy. He could see Tiffany going crazy here.

Tiffany enjoyed her view of Dexter across the table. They had each ordered a vegetarian sandwich, and were awaiting the order, each sipping green tea, sharing a passion for saving the earth and all that prowled it, and for denying themselves food that came from anything bearing the slightest mobility, be it camel or cockroach. Just as their waiter was leaning down above them to lower trays of food before each, out there on the sidewalk through the window, Tiffany was startled by a familiar figure walking by: *Troy?* Was that *Troy?* Her neck stiffened, her eyes dilated into radar as she gawked at the figure passing by.

"See somebody you know, Tiffany?"

Should she answer in the affirmative? And if she did, then she would have to bring Troy into the picture, and how risky this would be. Or simply lie.

"Yes," she answered, resetting her equilibrium, turning back to her tablemate. "A big surprise. I haven't seen her in ages, and I thought she had died."

Dexter said, "Maybe somebody else?"

"You might be right, Dexter." Tiffany tried to pull herself together. She smiled at her date. "How's your sandwich?"

"Divine!"

Oh, why did he use that word? Divine. A little too too. He must be. An image of Troy was storming her mind, and she had a hard time paying attention. If that were him she had seen through the window, surely he must be looking for *her*.

"And yours?"

Tiffany looked lost in her thoughts.

"And yours?"

The repeated question roused Tiffany back into the divine reality facing her across the table. "My sandwich is perfect, Dexter!"

Hold on, she told herself. Stay here, she added. In her frenzied mind, she was comparing the preppy Dexter to the surly figure she had just spotted passing along the street. She was overtaken by a desire to get her hands, as soon as possible, on the superior of the two. She wanted to run outside, and run after him. After this, she would do that. Run. She had already told Dexter, anyway, that she had a date to meet a friend in the afternoon.

Dexter gave her a nod, and she nodded back, all the while running by a vision of the shirtless Troy circling her bed ambivalently in the darkness of night, having come in, returning from nocturnal temptations, aimlessly, needing rest, maybe, or maybe only to stay for a while before returning to more chaos out there with someone yet to be known.

She threw off her wild preoccupation, and gave the young eager-eyed student across the way a reassuring smile. "It's a good day."

"It always is out here," he replied, feeling pleasantly connected, but for first time wondering about this new friend of his. Might she be a little — off?

Actually, she had taken steps to lay a mail trail for Troy, should he try finding her. She had given a forwarding address to her first apartment house manager and to her neighbor there, Maureen, telling them both to feel free to share the information with any of her friends from New York who might show up looking for her. In another few minutes, I'll remind Dexter of the date I have to meet Maureen. And then he'll be gone.

As Troy was walking down Broxton Avenue, he was struck by the profusion of youth, by the preppy shops, everything clean and bright, and all of it together composing the shining affluence of a prosperous upper New York state village. Somehow, he could not see Tiffany fitting in here. But there was that restaurant he had passed, the Good Earth that he could see her drawn to. He had almost gone inside to try one of the vegetarian sandwiches, but he was too anxious to find her address on Ashton.
  To get there, he had to cross vehicular mad Wilshire Boulevard, which felt like a freeway with crosswalks, and which made him feel like a lost cockroach scrambling for his life to scale it from one side to the other. A block later, he came upon Ashton, a tranquil street lined with a lovely blend of single-dwelling homes and small apartment complexes. Troy saw a plastic utopia of the sort against which Tiffany Orr would normally rail. She must not have lasted there very long, he guessed. Finding the address, he faced a leisurely layout of upscale one-story living units, spaciously separated and landscaped with healthy grass, sprinklers singing away, thop thop thop!
  He felt a rush of desire, neither exactly sexual but more than social, as he walked through an archway, up a long winding path graced with vines and roses, through small home-like apartments on each side, to the front door. He studied a listing of occupant names. Tiffany's was not among them. He pressed the button for unit 1, Manager. He waited and heard nothing. He pressed it again. Waited some more. Same silent reaction. Hell, what if she had moved back to New York?
  He turned in haste, reversing course and feeling rejected already. Maybe she had moved somewhere else, just to avoid him. On his way back to the front gate, on the path stood a young woman of no looks at all, seizing Troy's attention with a clutching smile.
  "You were looking for somebody?"
  "Tiffany. Orr."
  "Oh, sure," said the woman with the built-in look of a full-time loser. "She moved out last, when was it? Around March or April,

I'm thinking."

"Only a few months?"

"Not that long ago," she answered.

"Might you happen to know where she moved to?"

"Let me think," she said, giving him the eye.

Troy gave her a look mixing respect with feigned interest, something this homely female probably had a hard time getting from anybody, Troy figured.

She offered, "I knew her, a little. Holistic type? Tarot cards, massage?"

"Ah, yeah."

"That's Tiffany. Oh, wait. I think I know where she moved."

"You do?"

"Not far from here. I'm Joyce."

Her needy approach gave him the willies, but he half-smiled. "Troy."

"Follow me, Troy. I might have her address. I'm good at keeping track of friends. Like to stay in touch. In this world, you got to fight to find them, and it's even worse, keeping them."

It must be a near-impossible feat for her, he thought, especially the "keeping." Now what? If I can just get in and get out without losing it. Contain yourself, Troy told Troy.

He followed Joyce into her small tidy apartment, bracing for a clumsy campaign of unwanted charm and maybe even a clumsy strip tease. Actually, her place was more frugal than stuffed. On that count, one for her. It looked plain in a tasteful way, like a well-arranged display of unwanted items at a flea market.

"Wait there." Joyce went into another room, and came back a few minutes later, empty handed.

"Jeez," she said, pretending. "If the manager was in. Want something to drink?"

Troy balked. "Oh, no thanks."

"Sure is a hot afternoon. I might go out for a swim. Let me check some other places. Be right back. Sit down, take a rest!"

Reluctantly, Troy eased himself into a lone chair, wondering if he were the first person ever to pay it a visit.

The lonely woman opened a door up the hall to a walk-in closet, and looked inside, stalling for time. Her mind was plotting: How can I get him into my bedroom? Show some skin?

Flustered with desire, she loosened the top two buttons on her yellow blouse, and parted each side to expose what cleavage she could offer. Something like the size of two oranges in a Russian market. She felt sexy. They like that. Make it look easy. Money? Was he a hustler? Hmmmm ... she hated admitting to herself that she hoped he were. Then, maybe she could negotiate.

She came out of the closet, and walked back up the hall toward the visitor, yawned like a wicked woman. "Nothing there," she announced.

Troy saw through the come-on. "Okay, well thanks," he said, lifting himself from the chair.

"Wait! Hold on." I think I know the building where she moved to."

She pretended to be searching her mind. "Yes, it's on Hilgard."

"Hilgard? I think the bus came down that street."

"That's right. Only a block or two before Sunset."

"You don't have the number?"

"No, but ... yes, I do know that building, come to think of it. You can't miss it, reddish brick, two or three stories. Out front, there's this little statute of a lion."

"A lion."

"Somebody was talking about it the other day, wondering whatever happened to Ms. Orr."

Troy rose to his feet. "Thanks for that. I should be able to find it."

"I can go up there with you, if you want." Her eyes scanned his body like a medical device.

"Oh, that's okay, but thanks. I'll find it."

Joyce was not done with him yet. "Now hold on. If you have no luck up there, let me write down the manager's phone number."

"Sure, thanks."

Joyce found a pad and pen on the table and wrote out the number. "And, look. I'll give you mine, too, just in case?"

She looked up at him, hoping for a stronger face.

He nodded.

"You never know," she said. "I might find out something more. I know a lot of people who live here. Call the manager back later. Or me, if you like." Now, her radar eyes were shining. She was picturing him in the natural. Wait a moment, if only...

Troy flashed another fake smile. "Nice of you, Joyce."

Joyce felt a thrill, even if she'd stolen it. She had managed to extract a few stimulating words from the slender Adonis. Words she would take to bed with her later that night and make the most of. And, of course, put him at the top of her Wait List. And wait for the rest of her life for him to be desperate enough to call. And be ready to give him exactly what he would probably want. One of the advantages of her socially dead life was that she had saved up a lot of money. If only she could nail the right man to waste it on.

Joyce followed Troy out the door. "So, if you need anything, Troy, you know how to reach me." He remained non-committal, and she stood there, and drooled like a hopeless fan as he walked off, and waited, but then hurried up the path to study his figure vanishing under the archway and out onto the sidewalk. How she would love getting her hands on that. She could afford a half hour of prime time. Oh, God, how did Tiffany bring that off? Did she get him in bed? Joyce simmered with envy, and thought, I'm enrolling in foot massage school.

Troy walked back down to Wilshire, crossed it with recurring trepidation, and kept walking until he came upon Hilgard, then headed up the street towards Sunset.

Half a dozen blocks up, there stood a majestic little lion statue on the front lawn. Troy followed the foot path leading to the front door. He rang the manager's bell, and waited.

Out came a woman of large bulk, her face lathered in rouge.

"You're inquiring about the apartments?" she asked, gruffly.

"Not exactly," he answered. "I'm looking for a friend of mine, Tiffany Orr."

The assistant manager glared at him.

"I knew her back in New York," said Troy, pouring on the charm. "This was the address I had for Tiffany. I wanted to look her up."

"Wait there," said the woman, impatiently.

In fact, she had access, filling in for the vacationing Verla back in Oklahoma, to a phone number for Tiffany they had found in her apartment after she moved out. Verla didn't know the number's importance, if any, but, as usual, thought it a good idea to keep just in case. The renter of not even half a year had acted so erratic when confronted about there being another person living with her, that she became defensive, and vacated her unit in a couple of weeks.

While Troy waited outside, a young couple, as innocent looking as Sesame Street during a pledge break, came up the steps and went into the building. Whatever had attracted Tiffany to this picture-perfect neighborhood, Troy wondered.

The assistant manager returned, with a slip of paper in hand.

"Here, I don't know who Steven is, but he might know something about the woman."

"The woman" sounded like a snide put down.

"Do you recall when she moved out?"

"Oh, a few weeks ago. So, you know her well?"

"Yes."

"I see. Well, good luck."

The woman issued an obligatory grin, went back inside and closed the door.

Steven.

Who was Steven? Troy scanned his brain like a rolodex, feeling insecure as he walked down the steps and out onto the sidewalk, and headed up to Sunset to catch the next bus for Hollywood. Steven. Then, he remembered. Steven was probably the friend who had talked Tiffany into making the move to L.A. Steven was just a friend, or so that's what Tiffany told Troy. Now, he wasn't so sure, feeling the onset of jealousy. But he would call Steven. She may be living with him. It all felt suddenly promising, like many doors had been opened all at the same time. Lead by lead, he was that much closer. Yes, he thought, this place is one very big small town.

After freeing herself from Dexter's company, Tiffany walked in haste to Maureen's place on Ashton. Maureen might know, she hoped, if there had been any mail from New York for Tiffany that had come there since her move-out, and if it had been forwarded to Hilgard, or returned to the sender.

Maureen was happy to see Tiffany, the two settled into chairs overlooking the patio, and beyond that a swimming pool shared by surrounding apartments. They exchanged pleasantries, starting out with Maureen's ceramics. And then, Tiffany raised the subject uppermost on her mind; the letter. Maureen had not known of any letters, and so Tiffany gave her Steve's phone number, just in case a friend came inquiring.

"So, now," began Maureen, concealing her reservations about what she sensed Tiffany could not let go of, "if anybody comes around looking for you, you want me to give them Steve's number?"

"Yes," replied Tiffany, careful not to vacillate or to allow an opening for Maureen to raise the subject of the fellow who had abused her.

"Allright," said Maureen, the name Troy coming to mind. She would politely not ask Tiffany about Troy. "I don't know, Tiff," she said. "Maxie always forwards letters on. Maybe he sent a letter here. I could ask Maxie about it, after she returns from church."

They talked some more about Maureen's work and friends, and about her ceramic collection and Tiffany's so-called new screenplay in the works. Tiffany had a hard time staying focused, obsessing over the figure, so much like Troy, that she had seen out the window at the Good Earth. She wanted to be out on the streets, running up and down every one of them in search of the brooding poet whose free spirt and looks imprisoned her. No wonder she had been unable to write much since coming out to L.A. She had yet to find a way back to the stage where a writer gets up every morning, and writes.

Maureen was walking out with Tiffany up to the street to see her off, as Joyce, standing behind a drawn curtain, peered through.

"Keep me in mind for a movie!"

"I will. Wonderful seeing you, Maureen! I'll send you my number as soon as I move in, wherever that is!"

"If you do move into Encore, I'm expecting an encore over there!"

"That you shall receive!"

When Tiffany was gone, Joyce came running out.

"Maureen!"

Maureen stopped. "What's up?"

"A young fellow came around, about an hour ago, looking for Tiffany."

"He did?"

"Yes. I knew you were gone. I described the building up on Hilgard where Tiffany moved to."

"Oh, you did, "said Maureen, not knowing whether to laugh or regret Joyce's intervention. "How like a movie. Tiffany was just here. Did you get his name?"

"Troy."

Maureen could not resist. "Some people never learn."

Joyce made a face. Was Maureen casting aspersion on the fellow she had just entertained and was now desperately dreaming of spending more time with, somehow?

Joyce, one of the people who never learned, went back into her clean, spare unit, replaying in her mind the encounter with Troy. Hoping he would end up down and out, and in abject desperation would dial her number. She would be there to take it and to offer him whatever he needed. And to be wonderfully used. Now, on that alone, she could spend a lifetime waiting.

Wednesday morning laid a dark grey egg outside April's window. No trace of We-Love-You-LA anywhere in the dirty grey sky. It hung there, ominously close to Earth, as if conspiring to smash dreamland into a flattened junkyard. April wondered if MGM had shut down for the day, or it Paramount had blown a giant fuse. Maybe after a while, Mother Nature would come out of her sulk and lighten up and give the town the one thing that compensated for everything else wrong about it. April gazed through the window, searching for a trace of it anywhere.

She called Alex, wanting to run the Tiffany Orr application past him for a quick impression, just in case he thought they should pass on it and waste no more time. He picked up, and listened, and April gave him the basics, knowing he liked things as simply put as possible.

She said, "Only a few months at her last place. No lease."

"Well, it wasn't by the hour," quipped Alex.

April giggled with fluttery abandon. She knew how Alex enjoyed her giggles. "The one before that, six months. She might have gotten mixed up with a younger fellow on drugs."

"What young fellow is not?"

"The phone numbers she gave us all worked."

"So she's real, but a little flaky."

"Two employers said her work was good. No raves. She's doing secretarial temp jobs. Writes screenplays on the side."

"That's to be expected," said Alex, chuckling. "Look, okay, if you and Manny agree — I won't be back for another week — offer her for a six-month lease, plus first and last month's, plus $500 security. And here's a must, April. Now, tell her that if she wants to move in one of her young drugged out friends off the streets— no, don't say that. Said deadbeat will have to submit a separate application of his own. Stress his *own.* This can put a lid on riffraff fast, and if need be, we can evict sooner. If she accepts, and if Manny agrees, be sure he does, okay?"

"Yes, yes."

"Then, I can live with that."

"Okay, Alex, I will. I'll talk to Manny again."

"Good going. I'm in a hurry, you're doing a good job, kid."

"Thanks! Alex."

The phone clicked off.

April was up on her feet, re-energized, circling herself in the kitchen, making up her mind to cross the hall and confer with Manny.

The phone rang. Maybe it was Manny. She picked up.

"Hi, April!"

"Jerry!"

"You're up?"

"Having my morning tea, here under a cement sky."

"Smog again!"

"And we thought we were spoiled," said April. "Still, I have a lovely view out my kitchen window of Masterpiece Theatre. I'd kill to live over there."

"You'll have to show me that, sometime."

"I did already, when you were over."

"You did?"

"Right out the window."

"I must have been looking at you."

"Oh, don't flatter me, Jerry!"

"I can't help myself."

"It's hump day," said April, giggling. "Are you at work?"

"Yes, on a break, humping."

They laughed..

"Thought I'd ring you up."

"So, what's new? Anything exciting?"

"I had a dream..."

"Yes ..."

"Don't know if I should discuss it while at work."

"One of those?" No answer.

"A dream about?"

"Somebody new."

April's sailing spirit crash landed. He'd met somebody else.

"Tell me about her," she said, faking the good news as would a good friend.

"I can't now. At work. How about later? Can I come by? We can go somewhere to eat if you like."

"Sounds like a deal."

"I'll bring you some fresh day-olds!"

There was a knock on April's door.

"Okay, ah, somebody at the door, Jerry. Call me when you're getting off work!"

"About six thirty!"

"Bye!"

April rang off, and went over to open the door.

Out there stood Mister Depression Era Musical, prim and well-scrubbed and grinning like an oversexed prude trying to apply what he just read in a self-help book for the carnally challenged. Was there nothing Cecil could do in a natural way, April wondered.

"Good morning, Cecil!"

"I wanted to hand deliver my rent to our new house manager elect."

"Oh, thank you," said she, accepting Cecil's check.

Cecil admired April's twirling, if unexacting, sweep of blond hair. "You look camera ready for a Busby Berkeley production."

"Busby Berkeley," said April, thinking who Busby Berkeley was, then remembering.

"And what year are you thinking — 1929?"

Cecil laughed awkwardly, as if this, too, had been rehearsed.

"I have a certain golden age heroine in mind, and you're the perfect match."

"Round-faced Jean Harlow?"

"Yes, Harlow!" beamed Cecil.

April looked wary. Others had said the same thing, but Harlow, in April's opinion, had a weight problem, ill-suited to the red carpets of today's Hollywood.

"Harlow was a neon goddess," proclaimed the director-elect.

"In 1933."

Cecil chuckled, even this in a stentorian voice as stiff as redwood, thought April, amused by the deep timber of it. And she wondered how twisted up in social knots on the inside he might be. And felt like he deserved more from her.

"Come on in, if you wish," she offered.

"I'm flattered!"

He fairly danced into the room.

"Sit down, Cecil, please."

Cecil studied the cheerful space, feeling romance in the air. He'd never been inside before. "It's very like you in here."

"Pretty basic," she said, crossing to the stove to warm up the tea pot. Her mother had emigrated from England, and so she was raised in a half-English household, tea being a daily habit. "Tea? Coffee. Water?"

Cecil pondered.

"Sugar free diet water?"

Cecil squeaked out a tiny laugh.

"I'm open," he said, feeling as if he had arrived. Really, he was hoping to learn more about Pearl Dubuque, the older woman who lived in the building's only two-bedroom unit. He knew little about her other than rumors of her having been a minor, long-forgotten screen rival in the silent days of Gloria Swanson. That was enough to fire his imagination. He could imagine creating a role for the mysterious recluse in the new 1930's musical upon which he was slaving over, as if on a mission to reclaim a lost world.

"So how are things up there," asked April. "Any more noise bothering you from unit 10?"

"I've not been very bothered lately," he answered, giving April a leering eye of the Groucho Marx school, "but I've been bewitched and bewildered." He produced another squeaky laugh. April giggled half-heartedly.

"I am hoping to meet the lady upstairs."

"You mean Pearl Dubuque, Cecil?

Cecil beamed.

"Be prepared to hope forever," said April. "Pearl Dubuque's entire life is devoted to hating the one star she claims to have been her only competition on the silver screen."

Cecil came dramatically alive. "Gloria Swanson?"

"Norma Desmond," corrected April. "I've only met her a few times. Last one, oh yes, a leak in her kitchen faucet. Some leak. Manny and I couldn't find a drop. But I played with a wrench, turned it this way and that, made a big to-do about nothing. She bought the act."

Cecil applauded. "Kudos! When my plumbing fails me, may I come to you?"

April, surprised by the unexpected innuendo from Mr. Stentorian Victorian, laughed out loud.

"I don't do body parts," she said.

Cecil feigned rejection. "Drats!"

April giggled for the fun of it. "But I'm good with a wrench."

A look on Cecil's face.

"Don't say it!"

How I'd love to be wrenched by her, wished the private Cecil to himself.

April returned to the subject of the woman upstairs. "She rarely goes out. Manny might find a way of getting you in."

The telephone rang. April answered it. Manny was on the line.

"Oh, hello, yes," said April, her voice a little lower. "I haven't forgotten you. Company at the moment. Yes we will talk soon, this very evening. Okay."

She put the phone back to rest. She looked at Cecil and sighed with a smile. "It's Wednesday, isn't it? And I have some business to tend to, Cecil. Thank you for your check."

Cecil was up on his feet. "My monthly pleasure, April!"

Monthly pleasure. Is he for real, she wondered. "Do you like donuts? Day-olds?"

"I'm never one to pass up sweets from a sweet young lady."

Sweetness be damned, April wanted to scream.

"Here," she said, picking up the pink box half full of donuts and handing it to Cecil, "take them. They're yours."

"How grand! Are you sure you don't want any?"
"Oh, I can always get more. My boyfriend works at a bakery."
"Aren't you lucky!"
"Yes, especially my waist."
"Thanks for the drinks, April."
At least he didn't break out singing Tea for Two.
"Enjoy your day, Cecil. Are you working?"
"Taking a day off, pitching to producers."
"Hey, lots of luck with that!" If only he knew what he was up against in this town, she thought, stifling a laugh.

# CHAPTER 6

April waited a few minutes, and then went out and across the hall to knock on Manny's door. He opened it, and invited her right in. She sat down at the table, and showed him the revised rental agreement which she had prepared pursuant to Alex's instructions. "Second occupant must submit their own application."

"That's good." He read over it carefully.

"He said that if you and I agree, only then should we rent to Ms. Orr."

Manny crunched his face a little, torn between a woman he might have fun flirting with and the nagging scent of a problem tenant. But Ms. Orr's age worked in her favor.

"I think so, "he said.

"Are you sure, Manny?"

"We're covered with the second renter clause. So, we see if she can come with the deposit?"

"I have a feeling she will. She seems to have a friend, and she's got charm."

Many started to say, "Oh, does she ever," but caught himself. No, no, don't give away my lovely secret to April. "Okay," he said, instead. "I hope you're right."

"Okey-dokey," piped April, feeling relieved. "I'll give a call to her friend tomorrow morning. I have a date tonight.'

Manny's eyes brightened. "Who's the lucky fellow?"

"Your favorite candidate."

"I could see the spark of romance in your eyes, April!" he said. "And look what it does for your spirit. You're a woman in demand, getting swept up in the whirlpool of life. A good thing!"

April frowned. "Oh please."

"I see it. You can't fool me, girl. And he's not the only one, either."

"All right, so there's Mister Golden Age Musical, too. He was just down here asking about Pearl again. He's writing a new movie he thinks she would be perfect for."

Manny grinned. "Squaw Man, the Musical?"

They laughed.

"Okay, I'll see what I can do," offered Manny. "I have a gig up there tonight with our Norman Desmond. Need to get ready. A little shopping. She's expecting an overnight guest. But they never arrive until after she has gone to bed, or so that's what I tell her."

"A visitor? Whoever sleeps there?" She rose to leave.

"Nobody really," said Manny. "Just a reason to wash the sheets and remake the bed. And to set the table for three."

"Beyond belief," said April. "You are something else, Manny. See you later."

April slipped across the hall, and back into her unit. She picked up the telephone and dialed the hotel where Tiffany was staying, a little curious to scope out the operation. Here was an excuse.

After two rings, "Stargazer," growled a scratchy female voice.

"May I be put through to Ms. Orr."

"Who?"

"Ms. Orr".

"Or what?" said the voice, laughing. "Sorry, there, couldn't resist. Never heard of an Orr, except on a boat."

"You don't have an Orr registered?"

"I'll try Orr, doesn't raise my blood pressure, and, believe me, some of the names they pass through these doors do. Orr ... Tarter? Is Tiffany her first name?"

"Yes.

"Got a Tiffany Tarter?"

"I wonder if that's her," surmised April.

"Oh, yeah, I think I know that one. Fake blond type, middle age, willowy as a loose stem?"

April laughed. "Sounds like ours."

"And who are you? You have a sing-songy voice."

"Oh, do I? "said April, tickled. "I manage Encore Apartments."

"Encore? Love the name, honey."

"Oh, thank you. Yes, could you try your Orr — I mean ..."

"Tarter," said the front desk. "I would if I could, hon, but Ms. Tarter, or Orr, ha! Pardon me. That version of the woman checked out, I see, late last night. So I guess Ms. Orr's boat came in. But then again, knowing her, it may have gone right back out, and she'll be around again by nightfall, awaiting the next."

"Really?"

"She likes checking in or out. Let me see if she left something in storage. Hold on."

April waited a few moments.

The voice returned. "No evidence of Ms. Tarter's legacy in the hold bay, hon."

April was amused. "Are you a comedian? "

"Well, isn't it obvious, hon? Yes, I do stand up, but every time I stand up they tell me to sit down. Ha!"

"You shouldn't give up," April encouraged.

"You're a darling, dear, whomever you are."

"April."

"April. Lovely name. And I'm Helen. Come by sometime and we can continue that. Now wait, I'm thinking Ms Tarter, or Orr, left a contact number with our concierge, that's our elevator operator, and he may have put it into our rolodex, which I am now rolling. Tarter ... friend, it says: Steven Murdoch. Want it?"

"Oh, yes, I think I have the number, but I'll take it, just in case." Anything to prolong her amusing encounter with the front desk.

Helen gave the number, and April wrote it down.

"Thank you so much, Helen. It's been fun!"

"Yeah, let's do it again. This is a good time, before the traffic turns tense. Bye." The phone rang off.

April tried dialing Steve's number, but it was busy. It was almost always busy when she called. She gave it half an hour, and dialed again. Now, the answering machine kicked in, and she left the message: Your application has been approved
Done!
She turned her attention to the date with Jerry that evening, to the ever-agonizing subject of what to wear. But at least, the question faced her. She had to admit to herself, she did feel like a winner, what with Jerry and now Cecil Fanton.

Jerry finished up his day's work at the bakery, went into the restroom to change clothes, wipe his face with a warm cloth, comb his hair and practice smiling at April. He decided to be a little flirty, encouraged by the teasing tone of her voice when last they spoke. He could flirt and still show control. He knew she wanted that, conveyed by her wanting them to be "friends." But don't be too passive or polite, he reasoned, or she'll think I'm gay. Where to take her? He decided on a new, much-talked-about Thai place on Melrose Avenue.
He left the bakery with a pink box in hand.

Troy was out on the Santa Monica beach, waking up after a long sleep. Earlier that day, he had taken a bus out, wanting to see the famed Santa Monica pier, to hang out and size up the crowd, and to see how many heads he might turn. Very reassuring. He held his own swimmingly well in this crowd of the young and the old sharing the sand, some of them sleeping, others laying flat like mannequins in storage. He could see Tiffany fitting in quite well, for she sported a fetching aura neither cliché nor extreme, and managed to fool many people into believing that she was much younger looking than her actual age. His desire to see her again was hardening. Shirtless, he strolled across the sand as if he owned it, drawing widespread attention. He lay out under the sun and instantly felt like a sex object under ravishing surveillance. He could do alright for himself in this town if she were not here. Certainly, he could for a few weeks. He would consider it a vacation, and then, if he could not find her, maybe take a bus back to New York. Or maybe find somebody else. So many eyes. So many ways to wing it. The sand was soft, warm. I could sleep out here all night.

He was tired, and he dozed off, and lay there on the velvety sand for several hours. And when he awoke, the sun was slanting down toward the west. He wanted to come back. He walked along the esplanade, as picturesque as a post-card from the thirties. So this was La La Land. Now it was his, too.

On Wednesday evening, on trendy new Melrose Avenue, Jerry's eyes were locked on April's across the table they shared. Good Earth infidels, they shamelessly indulged in mini-mountains of noodles and rice and chicken, a veritable sugar festival without end. April warmed to Jerry's boyish attention.

"Whatever else on the menu you may want, April, this one's on me."

"Oh, no, you are spoiling me again, Jerry."

"Just by taking you out to dinner?"

"My self-control is shot for the evening."

"And mine, for the night," he said, thinking himself clever, but failing to get a rise from April. She was enjoying his easy company, but reminding herself of their having agreed to start out, rather than end up as they had laughingly reasoned, as friends. No wonder he had called me up about there being somebody new in his life. Friends share, and that's what he wanted to do. She did not wish to dwell on it. By the glow in his eyes, she wondered if he were merely trying to make her jealous. It was a reassuring thought to hold. The sound of the waitress pulled her out of her troubled thoughts.

"Like to see our deserts?' asked the lovely Asian server, smiling submissively in a suggestive whisper, as if about to massage either or both of them up onto the table for a happy interlude between the main course and killer pastries.

"Oh, desert, yes!" sang Jerry. The waitress went away to fetch them a menu. Jerry twinkled at April. "You too?"

"Me, too," replied April, admiring Jerry's strong shoulder blades.

Troy's sleep on the beach had been so rejuvenating, that he vowed to return to this new Eden the next day. He could even see himself spending a night here. Emboldened by all the heads he had turned, he boarded the number 4 bus, refreshed and ready to spend a little time in the hustling corridors of West Hollywood. And when the bus passed through, he gazed out the window at men scantily clad. He was not one of them. Not him. No. He knew all about the scene, however, having lived in the Village, where he learned, for reasons of convenient survival, to tolerate, when need be, almost every kind of behavior. At Crescent Heights, he got off the bus. Young skinny boys stripped to their waists stood aimlessly along curbs, waiting for cars to pull up alongside, their doors to open, small talk to proceed: Are you a cop? No, said the other. And are *you* a cop?

Troy walked easy on Santa Monica, feeling confidently connected. He had friends in Manhattan who dealt drugs and, on the side, turned tricks for money. Not here, he vowed—unless all else fails. He could do it, but he hated doing it. A more promising possibility, he had heard of rich, aging women hiring young men for company, to drive them around and take them to restaurants. No, don't go there, he thought, focusing on the good days with Tiffany.

At the busy corner of Santa Monica and La Brea, he asked an ill-kempt kid, "Any good straight bars around here?"

The kid, composed of a bony frame, pock marked face topped with an unruly tangle of linty hair, gave him a keen reply. "Straight bars, maybe some of those down on Sunset; that's where the women work".

"Hookers?"

"Yeah, in drag. But there's a cool place, mixed crowd, called Circus Disco."

"Oh, yeah?" Troy fell into feeling already like a big brother to the kid, even if only a few years separated the two.

"It's only five or six blocks east of here, but on a side street. I'd draw it out for you if I had a pencil."

"That's okay," said Troy, pointing his finger east as a question.

"Yeah," said the kid. "Look, I'm going down there, anyway, to look up a friend. If you want, I can show you how to find the side street."

"Sure."

The lights on La Brea turned green, and they crossed.

"I'm Rusty," announced the boy.

"Troy." This one little encounter made LA feel as if it had opened up to him. And it helped him stop fretting over who Steven was.

The darkness was falling, and when the darkness fell in this town, it took on the vacant air of abandoned civility.

Wednesday evening at Pearl Dubuque's looked like an out-take from the making of *Sunset Boulevard.* Manny had been summoned to the Encore's largest apartment, the outlandish decor helping him to play the role of stern live-in butler, Max von Mayerling, without breaking up. Pearl's place was an out-of-control collection of stuffed pillows, vanity mirrors, gothic knickknacks, and overwrought figurines crowed together between oppressive objects of furniture that spelled Transylvania, The Kitsch Tour.

Manny rather enjoyed playing his role in the charade, and for his performance, he counted on the money she would give him now and then, ostensibly to help him out with his living expenses. Manny could not live on the meager social security he received from "Sammy," his nickname for Uncle Sam. Another path to Dubuque's charity were the rides he took her out on in his showy Buick, acting as chauffeur whenever the mood struck her to launch another "come back" campaign. Manny at the wheel. Dubuque alone in the back seat, imperially perched, head frozenly forward, as they cruised slowly up to the front gates of Paramount — slow enough to make some kind of an impression before being told her name was not on the list and that, unfortunately, she could not be let through to see Mr. DeMille, who, by way, sad to tell you, died about twenty years ago. "Oh, did he? What a shame, and it passed me by! Well, then I'd like to pay Warren Blinking a visit."

"Mr. Blinking. Oh yes, he retired back in 1969."

She would roll her eyes in mock disbelief. She would motion to Manny, who knew the drill. He would slowly back her up, the Buick that is, nod elusively to the gatekeepers, to pause and let anxious sight-seers gather around for a peak of a real movie star, some believing they were glimpsing golden age royalty, then slowly drive off, his gaze forward, steady.

"Never cast a glance at a commoner, Manny," Dubuque had instructed him. "That makes you one of them, and we are not one of them."

She would be perched on the back seat, recreating her perch from days gone by (actual or fantasized) on her way to a morning shoot. In her ears, all around were idolatrous fans shouting, "Pearl! Pearl! Pearl!" And studio-trained blue birds were chirping in rare harmony as they swept down to circle her automobile in aerial adoration. The scene worked well enough to placate Pearl Dubuque's out-of-order ego, even when she and Max were ignored by virtually everyone at the front gate. Once in a while, they might hear whispers – "Who is that? I've seen her in films, haven't I?" or "Look! There she is, still alive! Oh, maybe she'll make another film!"—rumored whispers, possibly staged by prearrangement between Manny and somebody at the front gate. Money changed hands in this town to sustain a thousand obsolete delusions.

Pearl Dubuque was no Gloria Swanson, hardly better than Marion Davis on a good day (with voice syncing). And contrary to the bloated bluster of Pearl Dubuque, swallowed by a few self-deluded fans of the silent era determined to bring it back, Swanson's star had eclipsed the light bulb of Pearl's discount aura many times over. But, oh, the redeeming solace of self-deception witnessed by fraudulent complicity.

Tonight, as in now, as in present tense on this very page, Dubuque was waiting for her Mayerling to arrive with "fan letters" just received, courtesy of Manny having the key to Dubuque's mail box so that he could fetch and deliver her mail to her each day. Actually, the "letters" had arrived decades earlier, but Manny, on the sly, had taken them from Dubuque's colossal collection and then, downstairs in his apartment, doctored the dates into the present tense. Dubuque never questioned telltale marks of deception. She knew better. Upstairs at the door, Manny arched his back, assumed the von Mayerling stance, and knocked with precision.

And waited, with precision.

Moments passed. He expected moments to pass. That was the way with stars in this town. For Pearl, Manny was the only person whom she could keep waiting. And through the door's peephole, she doted on watching him wait.

Finally, the door opened, by a crack.

"Yes, did Madam call?"

"She did, Manny."

The door opened fully. Manny strode through with the arch of a four-star general.

"And what is Madam's wish this evening?"

"Letters, Manny, you told me I have more from the fans. "

"Indeed, you have."

"But I only want the best three or four of the bunch. Remember, just the pearls for Pearl."

"Of course, Madam. I have screened them carefully."

He handed her two notes — minus envelopes. She took them to a chair beneath a lamp, and sat down. Manny followed her over and stood above, guarding her self-infatuation.

Beginning to read the first fan letter, the ancient star beamed.

"This is priceless, Manny. Please, read it for me!"

She handed the note back to her Max von Mayerling.

Max von Mayerling read, "My dearest Pearl ...."

"Oh," sighed somebody's dearest Pearl, "those words — he already has me in his hands."

"*She*," corrected Manny, deviously tickled with his offbeat sense of humor, although he suspected that Dubque, like so many leading ladies of the day, had also, if not exclusively, gone for other leading ladies.

"She? All right." She regrouped, her vanity unmolested. "I can play that side of the street too, Manny."

Daring to go tender on the wrong gender, Dubuque whispered, "She is worthy, Max. Read on..."

"How I lie anxiously awake some nights, dreaming of your beauty drawing achingly close."

"They could never get enough."

"They never could, Madam," echoed Manny, in von Mayerling's grave tones. Manny had set the stage exactly as expected by the lady upstairs. This would be a very good evening; the two were theatrically in sync, and he could expect a big payout, he felt sure.

"And the guests for tonight, Manny?"

"Buster?"

"Allright," she nodded, having wished for somebody more current.

"And maybe Billy."

"Oh, Billy. Didn't I tell you he would eventually call?"

Manny nodded, not pointing out that Billy was not Billy Wilder. Let her dream. Anyway, she would, taking the cue, not stay up late enough to receive the "guests," whomever they weren't.

"Yes. We'll play gin rummy tonight!"

"Of course we will. But he may be a little late, Madam."

"Read on, Manny."

Manny continued with a letter originally sent to her in 1928.

In her apartment the following morning, April was basking in the afterglow of her date the evening before with Jerry. Savoring, still, the sweet Thai cuisine. Outside the window, yesterday's cement sky had melted into glimmering blue. April was savoring her revised regard for Jerry's upper body, and she wondered how long she could keep up the pretense of being just friends. And then, she dreaded the thought of messing up a good thing. "Take it slow," her inner coach was saying. "Tell May it can wait, June, to hold that thought. July — go to hell." "Yes, she roared back, "I'm holding out for August this year!"

Through her kitchen window, she drank in the wondrous view of the mansion's lush lawns and shrubbery, so well and quietly kept, and assumed its aloof occupants must be spending their luxuries outdoors in the private backyard. If only she could get an invite over there. She might ask Jerry for ideas; perhaps a solicitation at the door with a pink box of fresh donuts made In Glendale.

But a question pricked April Downing's euphoria, like a tiny pin bringing down a Macy's Day parade balloon: Why had he been so flip in asking me to go home with him? She glanced down upon the pink box he had given her on their way home, a growing symbol of affection and longevity. A welcome surprise it had been, for Jerry had kept it concealed until dropping her off. Should I feel flattered, or insulted? He must be wanting to fatten me more. And, now he's hinting about somebody else being special in his life? Good grief, she thought, glaring with newfound suspicion upon the pink box, am I being punished?

She picked it up, intent on walking it back to the laundry room for others to share. But, would getting rid of it breach the warm feeling between herself and the baker boy? No, No, she wanted to shout: I refuse to join Whale Nation!

The telephone's shrill ringing called her back.

"Hello?"

"Have I reached April?"

Tiffany's bubbly voice. "Thank you for the message! I am floating!"

"Enjoy the float!"

"From your message, my search may be over!"

"Well I hope it is," said April. "We will need to go over the rental agreement with you, as soon as you can drop by."

"I can drop by in an hour."

"Perfect. And, oh yes, Tiffany, do you use another last name?"

"I do, for my writing. Tarter."

"As in tartar sauce?" April giggled.

"Oh, yes, for my writing. Does it zing?"

"Very zingy and saucy," said April. "Okay, then we'll see you in about an hour."

After the phone call, April dialed up Manny, to notify him of the imminent visit.

"Okay, I'll be there," he said.

April's phone clicked off, and Manny's dormant hormones clicked in, directing him to his bathroom and then to the clothes closet. This he did, going to work on his visage in the mirror, like a man preparing for a face lift. Shaved closer than usual. Snipped away some unsightly hairs from places where hairs should not be unsightly. Pushed through the closet like an English fop dressing up to meet the Queen. Give it my best, he thought. Somebody like this one doesn't come along every day. Middle age and in shape. Loads of charm. A tease, I can have a jolly good go around with that. He believed she had flirted with him. In fact, almost every man whom Tiffany met was left feeling he had been flirted with.

He chose tan slacks and a floral shirt. His big fantasy would be to drive off with Ms. Tiffany Orr seated next to him, the top down, and Pearl Dubque looming over it from her balcony above, gawking at her latest rival for von Mayerling's devotion being whisked away, up the street. At the moment, he was blooming mad over Dubuque's having, the night before, slipped into his coat pocket only two twenties. Bloody insult! Usually, she favored him with sixty or seventy, sometimes a nice hundred. All in the spirit of one friend helping another. And he had also done her laundry yesterday. Plus, in order to give evidence to the promised visit of Buster Keaton, Manny had spent ten dollars of his own on flowers, which Pearl would find the next morning on the table, having been told that, yes, Buster did come by, but after she had fallen asleep. How disappointed he was to have missed you!

He worked on what remained of his hair, moving each strand, one at a time, this way or that in a vain attempt to conceal a naked crown. Why did I have to grow old?

About an hour later, Manny was seated at the table in April's place, happy to be facing Tiffany Orr on the other side, while April was explaining the terms of the rental agreement. All seemed to be going well, until April got to the clause about a second tenant needing to fill out a separate application. Tiffany's ebullient spirt tripped and near fell.

April, nonetheless, held a steady professional demeanor. "We just need to be sure of who we are renting to. We've had some problems in the past with renters bringing others in without our knowledge."

"Of course," said the applicant, "I can appreciate your concern." She was picturing in her scheming mind the back stairs leading conveniently out to the back door, as she had recalled. A good escape route for late night visitors.

April turned to her cohort. "Can you think of anything else, Manny?"

Manny turned to Tiffany, "Did we tell you that our studios do not come with parking spaces?"

"Perfectly okay. I don't have anything to park!"

They laughed, and April felt relieved. "Okay. So, I think we've covered everything."

Tiffany rose. "Wonderful! I should have the money by, let me think. How about, by Friday at the latest?"

"No problem" said April, wondering if Tiffany really had the money. "We can hold it until then."

April walked Tiffany to the door. Smiles and good byes, and Ms. Orr was on her way. The vacant unit upstairs was now about to take on a new tenant. Its exorcized bath tub ready to accept and coddle the civilized world back into its ivory graces.

April settled into the arm chair. "So, now what do you think, Manny?"

"She wants it, but, by the look on her face, I don't know if she can produce the money. She only works part time."

"I wondered about that, too," said April. "But she didn't look very happy with the second occupant app, either."

"No, she didn't," agreed Manny. "I watched her face go from a bubble to a mud pie."

The amused April sprang to her feel in a whirl of giggles, and went to the stove to reheat the kettle for more tea.

"And why are you so decked out, Manny? Are you driving Dubuque around town today?"

"Oh, don't mention that fig. I was up there last night, gave one of my best."

"And?"

"Almost nothing in return, the old goat!"

"Show business can be cruel."

"Has she been asking you about Nick Petrini?"

"Hick Petrini? Are you kidding?"

"I think she heard him singing down the stairs. He sings in piano bars, you know."

"Yes, but she won't get anywhere with him." April rose. "Want some more tea, Manny?"

"Ah, yes. The perfect morning. Thank you."

Thinking well of April and the baker boy, Manny's mind was pulled back to his late wife. She had been the luckiest draw of his life, and he felt a sting of guilt over his silly Orr designs. He should give them up. He hoped the applicant might flake out. The friendship with April was all he needed. She would entertain him with a more pleasant vision of young love.

.

# CHAPTER 7

As the morning approached the noon hour, Troy woke up in a strange bed, looking around at strange walls, at a large vanity mirror on the ceiling. Where the hell was he, he wondered? And on such a large mattress, he felt like he were lying out on the beach, all alone in a world of insipid wealth. Away from Hollywood.

How had he ever ended up here? Had somebody driven him out here, and how far away was he from back there? He remembered going to the disco, as large as the roller rink in Brooklyn, the lights nearly blinding him, and of the kid named Rusty buying him a drink, it seemed, and of moving around dizzily through the crowd, being groped and hustled and feeling like a starving poet exposing his corrupt side, and of hearing "Shame" being sung over and over again, and somebody shoving a drink into his hand and insisting he cooperate, laughing as he did, and then being taken off with some people to ... where? Was he now confusing a fast evaporating dream with the strange setting in which he now found himself? Oh, of course, he thought, I'm waking up to a common hangover. Somewhere. I got drunk back there. Was it that kid who brought me here?

He looked around. Is he here, too? What was that kid's name? He saw his pants slumped over the end of the long bed. He sat up and reached for them, to go through the pockets and maybe find a note in a pocket helping him figure out how he had gotten here. On one of the slips of paper was Steven's phone number. He would try calling the guy. His only hope of finding, who? Who was he trying to find? Oh yes, Tiffany.

Wherever he was, he would have to get up from the bed, slip into his clothes and head back for Hollywood. The town was starting to feel like a home away from home.

The room looked like something you'd expect to find a studio chief living in. These are rich people. Who are they? Oh, that woman who hovered around me. A faint memory was starting to form, and he heard music droning on from somewhere else in the house. It sounded like Circus Disco. Enough of that. He pushed himself off the bed, crossed to the windows and looked out upon something suspiciously unreal: a clinically manicured garden that looked permanently unlived in. What the heck — a stage set? Am I on a stage set? Is this real? Am I dreaming this? Am I being secretly filmed? Go back to bed, me, go back to sleep, and make another wake up. I don't sleep walk.

Back onto the giant mattress he lay.

Footsteps sounded from another room.

He listened.

A dreamy female figure, neither young but impressively not old-looking, entered the room — her? Quietly possessive.

"So, you did manage to wake up before the clock struck midnight," said the intruder, smiling down upon him as if the two had been an item for years and were now facing a new day together, set pattern, set dialogue.

"What time is it?" he asked.

"Five minutes until," answered the visitor. "You made it again."

Again? That means we've shared this same experience before, and where?

The sensitive intruder glanced down upon his body as if to be verifying its condition, in preparation for putting it to some use.

Is he ... Where is he? Who is that up there looking over me like an admiring floor warden in a detention house?

He does not know what to say, the intruder's manner is so surreal that the show alone fixates his willingness to participate. Besides, he can feel a poem taking force in his disoriented mind. He will keep it a secret for now.

"So," where am I, he asked, gazing up stupidly at the voluptuous figure of an aging woman still attractively confident of herself. She is sitting casually on the far edge of this giant mattress.

"In my home," she answered, smiling.

"How did I get here?"

"My chauffeur drove us here. You don't remember?"

He looked all around, confused. "No."

She is sitting there in a composed manner.

"Are we in Hollywood?"

She surveys her anonymously forgetful conquest, rises and looks down upon him with blasé chagrin.

"No," she answers.

Troy rose to re-remove himself from the bed. "May I ask," he started. "Ah, sorry for not remembering, how did I meet you?"

"How did you meet me? You mean, how did I meet you?"

"All right. Oh, I know ..." He was slipping into his trousers, now wide awake. "Did I see you at the disco, back there?"

"Yes, and I approached you, back there. There was a boy with you, back there, and so I wondered."

"The kid, Rusty."

"Whatever. I smiled. You smiled back, back there. The usual start up. We talked a little. You were looking for a friend from New York, you said."

"Yes."

"And you looked so down. One thing lead to another. The usual. A drink as others danced. And then we left."

"Just like that?"

She paused impatiently. "You showed me a semblance of, shall we say, functional interest." She wanted to laugh. "You're in the Valley."

"The Valley?"

"San Fernando. It's not really as chic as it may appear out the window. All of that out there is the work of a set decorator, an old friend of a friend of ... another friend, not sure ...of mine."

Troy walked to the window. "I was looking out there, confused."

"You were. Maybe you were still asleep."

Troy watched her coming closer, now reaching out to politely touch the pure glassy skin of his unclad upper body. Wrong move. In the light of day, her slackening anatomy disappointed. Put the illusion at risk.

Insulted, she pulled away.

"Sorry," he said. "I'm still waking up."

"No need to feel anything, at all," she said.

"And I have to make a call."

"Of course you do."

"Somebody I promised to see."

"Of course you did. Soon?"

"It looks like afternoon out there. I should be returning, this is not Hollywood?"

"Far from."

"There's a bus near?"

"There always is," she said. "But that won't be necessary. I'll have my man drive you in."

Troy looked uneasy. "You know, how embarrassing this is. I don't remember your name."

"Of course, you don't. We met under noisy circumstances. I will write it onto a piece of paper, along with my phone number. I found you to be a perfectly suitable young man, I surely enjoyed myself, even if you slept through it all. As long as you don't feel offended, or overly taxed?"

"Oh, not at all."

"Well, then, just in case, maybe we can be sort of friendly, you never know, right?"

"Right," answers Troy, careful to preserve all options.

She sat down at a small table and wrote out her name and number, and he went over to be polite enough to reciprocate by accepting it. The name surprised him.

"Deborah. Have I heard that name somewhere?"

"Probably not. I don't use my real name, it can be difficult when somebody compares me to another, much younger image."

"You ... were ... a movie star?"

She smiled, non-committal. "And you were, Troy?"

"You remembered."

"At my age, I can't afford not to, Troy."

She walked him into the other room, called for a man named Art, who presently appeared, filling up space like a well-scrubbed trash can, at least gleaming, and instructed him to have the car waiting outside. The trash can removed itself.

Deborah watched as Troy hustled into the rest of his clothes and slipped into his shoes. She showed him to the door, and waited there for the car to come, and said, "Have a nice day in Hollywood with your friend."

He made a mischievous grin. "Sure, I think I will ... Deborah. And, ah, thanks!"

He got into the car, and off he was driven.

Troy mulled over the incredible night. She saw right through me. She doesn't buy my meeting a friend.

Looking out the window at an endless maze of newer Valley homes and little innocuous strip malls at every other intersection, he was wishing he had found Deborah more attractive, for he liked her suave manner. This should inspire a poem, he told himself. Suave. But, not a poem he would dare show Tiffany. Back there in Deborah's strange place, it felt like being in a play. As if it had been scripted. He could overlook the age, if need be. The slip of paper with her phone number on it might come in handy. A place to crash. Had she given him anything? He reached into his front pocket. Nothing. Into the other pocket. Nothing. Then, he leaned onto his left side and felt a bulge in his back right pocket. Yes, there it was, she had. And what a gratuity! He would count it up after being dropped off in Hollywood. And then decide how attractive he could talk himself into believing she were.

He would call Steven from a pay phone. The summoned car crossed the Cahuenga pass, and glided down Highland into Hollywood. Waiting for the lights to change at Franklin, the driver glanced around at him.

"Were do I let you out?"

"Anywhere is okay."

The driver crossed Hollywood Boulevard and pulled over at the end of the next block, next to Hollywood High. "This okay?"

"Thanks," said Troy, jumping out, a free man again, and with three hundred dollars in his pocket. Boy, do I still have it, he told himself, starting to feel a certain attraction to Deborah, and who did she look like?

That Thursday early evening, after Steven returned home from work, he listened, only half interested now, to a message from Mack, apologizing for having stood him up, if, in fact, that's what he had done. Mack took flakiness to new levels. But, it didn't matter as much to Steve now. He was filled with the joy of knowing, that now, there might well be a reconciliation between himself and Gary.

After the message ran out, the phone rang. Maybe it was Mack. He picked up.

"Hello?"

Street sounds. Arguing male voices ... cars streaming by.

"Hello?"

The connection died.

Steve dialed up Mack, waited for the beep, and left a message telling Mack that all was forgiven, and that, yes, he would be coming by later that night for the two to take in a movie. He went into the bathroom to take a fresh shave, to sharpen the shape of his hair, to rub a warm cloth over his face and test the state of its current condition in the looking glass. The phone rang. His heart rose. It must be him.

"Hello?"

"Is this Steven?" The unfamiliar voice sounded evenly masculine, composed.

"Yes.".

"I'm a friend of ..."

Other voice: Who you talking to?"

Caller to somebody else: "I won't be long, guy!"

Caller back to Steven: "Sorry. A friend of Tiffany's."

"Okay," said Steve, "I know her. So what's up?"

"I was out to her old place in Westwood. They said she moved, gave me your number."

"Oh, they did," said Steve. "I don't think I got your name?"

Another voice: "Peddle your ass somewhere else!"

Caller to somebody else: "Shut the!" ... back to Steven, "Ah, hello?"

"Yes," answered Steven, excitedly intrigued.

"Sorry for that. I'm Troy."

Troy. Who was Troy? Tiffany had never mentioned a Troy.

"I just got in town, from New York. I was calling to see if you might have a number for Tiffany."

"Only an old number, guy, if you want it."

"Anything."

"She's in-between apartments. Oh wait. I think I have her most recent number.?"

"Anything."

"Hold on."

Steve brought his address book to the phone. "Got a pencil?"

"Yes. I'm ready."

He read the number for Troy.

"Thanks, Steve. Do you know where she's moving to?"

Keep it vague, thought Steve, ambivalently, but give him some clues to work with. "I think she found a place down around the La Brea Tar pits."

"Around the tar pits?"

"Yes, well no. Not in them." Steve couldn't help laughing. "Near them, I mean. The pits are next to a big art museum. Tiffany might be renting on a street down there called, what was it — Rose or Spring, or, no, maybe Encore."

"Encore."

"Yeah, something like that."

Steve liked Troy's sulky voice, wondering what he looked like.

"I might have something if you call back in a few days."

"Cool," said Troy, sensing interest on the line. "Tell her, if you see her, I'll be in touch."

"I will."

Steve hung up, wondering why Tiffany had never mentioned a friend named Troy? Strange. He hurried out of his apartment, and went down to his car to drive off to Mack's place. And only a few minutes later, the telephone rang. Steve's greeting played out, and a caller came on to leave a message. "Steve. This is Gary. Yes, me. I know, it's been a while. And, I've been thinking about you. In fact, I never stopped."

Tiffany called Steve later that night, to ask if he could loan her a hundred dollars for the deposit, to which he quickly agreed. Steve gave her the message from Troy, and told her of his having given Troy her last phone number, and it was all she could do to conceal her elation. She felt like a reborn woman ready to roar again, to parade and be seen a victor in love, however contrived or self-subsidized it might have to be. It was in the stars, all aligned perfectly, she was certain. She had far more faith in the stars than she had in Sunday school. Fated, simple as that. Leave the tarot cards out of it on this one, she vowed. Steve took the high road, deciding not to tinge her momentary high with details of everything else he had heard in the background during the phone call.

Friday morning found Tiffany in high-gear. She had managed to raise the additional two hundred dollars she needed for the security deposit, one hundred each from Steve, who was overjoyed to be sharing with her the news of his having heard from Gary, and from her employer as an advance. She called April, excitedly to announce that she would be coming by during her lunch break, with the deposit. April was both pleased and cautious. By now, she was slightly on the fence, but there was no turning back, unless Ms. Orr could not deliver on the full deposit.

"So, then," Tiffany inquired, can I move in tonight?"

"Of course you can!"

"I have a good friend who will be driving me and my things over. I travel light, wait and see."

April felt reassured by Tiffany's having a friend who owned a car, and lied. "What a dream tenant you already are! Some people bring a whole museum with them."

"My life is a cardboard box!"

After ending the call, Tiffany rang up Ma Bell to place an order for a new telephone, and to arrange for people calling her old number to get a message referring them to the new number.

Later that afternoon, she checked out, once more, of the socially challenging Stargazer Motel. Steve was parked in his car outside, waiting to load what little she had into the back seat. The rest of her frugal possessions, which had been stored at Steve's apartment, were now in the trunk.

Steve drove west on Sunset, turned left on La Brea, and they talked about Gary. Steve had called him, and the two talked for over an hour.

"So, you two are going to get together in some way?" asked Tiffany.

"Oh yes, he offered to take me to dinner at a great place in Pasadena, tomorrow."

"Wonderful."

Tiffany said what needed to be said, feeling a sharp envy. She might not see as much of Steve if he and Gary got back together.

"Can't wait to see the place, Tiff," he said, glancing out the window at hustlers loitering about on La Brea and Santa Monica.

As Steve drove, he wondered if Tiffany's friend from New York was gay or "bi," as many men unable to out themselves wished to be known. And then, he caught himself ogling over another man along the street, and, thinking of Gary, felt a twinge of guilt. He hoped Tiffany had not noticed his distraction.

On Friday evening, Manny was upstairs in Tiffany Orr's unit, giving it a last look-over. When he was about to leave, he heard the door across the hall opening. He went up to the peephole to look. A heavy-set man toting a large camera strung over his shoulder came out of the unit occupied by Wayne and Melissa. Such a large camera. Maybe he had screen tested Melissa for some kind of a role, or a commercial. But why at her place? Manny waited a moment, and then left the apartment and walked slowly down the hall.

He spotted a business card at the top of the staircase. He picked it up. Dreamland Films. Justin Chance, Producer 818-492-6969. P.O. Box Reseda CA Suite 909. On it was written an address on Sherman Way in Reseda.

Now, what is this all about, he wondered, thinking the worst. The Valley — land of "Adult" cinema. Maybe a good reason for him and April to drive up there and check out the address, all, of course, in the name of responsible problem-tenant monitoring.

He hurried down to April's apartment to show her the card. He discovered her in the hall, talking to Tiffany and, apparently, to Tiffany's friend who had driven her over.

"It's all in the trunk of Steve's car," said Tiffany. She gave Manny a big gracious smile. "And how are *you*?"

"Hello again," said her new secret admirer. "Nice to see you. Your new home upstairs is in good order, and we are standing by to help, if need be."

"I'm glad you're standing by! Manny, this is Steve."

Steve said, "Nice to meet you, Manny."

Manny smiled. "The pleasure is mine."

"Tiffany travels light, Manny."

"How much easier life is that way."

"So, follow me," said April. "I'll take you upstairs!"

"Lights! Camera! Action!" proclaimed Steve.

Upstairs in the studio, Steve surveyed, with misgivings, the few pieces of furniture that made it, technically, a "furnished." But Tiffany was in her comfort zone in old places like this that felt tentative and a little dark. She was sure that Troy would be turned on, too, for the same reasons. And how easier for intimacy to arise, giving the confining space. No other rooms to run to.

April entered, to tell Tiffany of having some extra chairs and a small table in the storage room, if she were interested.

"Yes!" replied Tiffany. "Maybe something I could set my typewriter on, and over here," she said, crossing to the far side of the room, "against the window. I can look out."

Down there, looking up in her direction, stood a familiar figure. Might it be him? She turned away, her heart beating.

"I think I may have just the thing, Tiffany," announced April, leaving the room.

Tiffany turned to Steve, "Do you like it?"

"It's so you."

"It is."

"How's the bed, have you tried it?"

"I did. I'll show you."

"Not necessary. I know how they work, Tiff. I'm taking a look at your kitchen."

While Steve was in the kitchen, Tiffany walked over to the window, and looked down.

Good. He's gone.

Steve came back into the room. "What are you looking at?"

"The white building across the driveway."

"What's it for?"

"That's what I'd like to know. Strange."

Steve joined her for a peak. "All white. Looks like a lab."

April returned, followed by Manny, the two bringing into the room a small book case.

"Oh, that's nice," said Tiffany. "Thank you!"

She looked around. "How about over there against the wall?"

Manny and April placed it by the wall.

"Couldn't find the small table, Miss Tiffany." said Manny. "I'll keep looking."

"Come on, Tiffany," said Steve "A few more boxes to bring up."

April and Manny followed the two downstairs. "If you need anything, just ring or come down and knock."

"Thanks."

She and Steve went down to his car to bring up the rest.

"Love the area," said Steve, "After this, we go to Pinks! I'll have a hot dog. You can have relish with pickles on the side."

"You are so funny," said his vegetarian friend, and then, jolted with fear, she spotted a male figure up the street. That's no him, is it?

Up on Sunset Boulevard, Troy was standing at a pay phone in front of a rundown little motel, trying to make up his mind. Should he call Deborah? Just one more night, and then he'd have more money to spend on Tiffany. He felt a gentle tap on his shoulder.

"Hey, is that you, guy?"

It was Rusty. "Where have you been, Troy? See, I didn't' forget your name, did I!"

Troy warmed to the sight of the kid. "Hey, what's been happening?"

"Just making ends meet."

So far, Troy had not called the number given to him by Rusty.

"Did you find a place to stay, guy?" asked the kid.

"Oh, here and there," answered Troy, seeing Rusty as a younger brother and wanting to set a better example.

Rusty studied the uncertainty in Troy's eyes. "You can always crash at my place."

"And who's there besides you?"

"Nobody. The owner lets me stay, just to keep an eye on it. Security in the building is a joke. He only uses it during the day for filming."

"Meaning, what?"

"Porno."

"So when do you think you'll be back there?"

"I can go there now, show you were it is. I got money in my pocket."

"So do I, "said Troy. "Okay, so show me your pad, kid. I'll give you some money to help out."

"It's free."

"So, let me buy you something. Cigarettes, booze? ... a teddy bear?"

Rusty laughed. "If that makes you feel good."

Troy saw a real person. He wondered why the kid had ever ended up here, and then he wondered about himself, too. And then, looking at Rusty, he wondered if the kid was thinking sex.

"Look, " began Troy, "you're not wanting to..."

"Don't worry. We can be friends."

Troy relaxed, feeling suddenly like he were going home. "Okay, I'm beat. Take me there."

"But will you get me that teddy bear on the way?"

Troy grinned: "How many inches?"

Rusty laughed, and so did Troy, one of the few times he had laughed since arriving in the City of Angels. They headed east on Santa Monica Boulevard, happily ignoring all of the hustlers passing by. And the Johns in their cars. Happily giving over the night to others, their camaraderie spelling out, "closed for the evening."

That evening was a big evening for Jerry and April. They were dancing up a storm in a little hole-in-the-wall not far from where Jerry lived on Peach Grove Street, off Vineland. By the way April was carrying on, nobody would ever take her for the platonic type, not on the tiny dance floor that buzzed and bristled with patrons in various stages of inebriation, venting their physical natures to the music of Boy George, Heatwave, and the Jackson Five. Elsewhere in the cozy little club, others were tossing darts, and there was a pool table in full use. Many at the bar looked half stoned.

April felt luckily connected to the scene, for Jerry kept his adoring eyes on her — so far – and she, to her surprise, on him. The tight-fitting black T shirt he was wearing flattered his firm arm muscles. Had she failed to notice them in the beginning, or was her mind playing tricks on her?

Jerry shouted through the grinding soundtrack, WHAT DO YOU THINK OF THIS PLACE?

She shouted back, FUNKY FUN! She tossed him a wayward grin, the alcohol melting away her daytime restraint.

A new song that sounded faintly from another era was jamming the air:

> We're steeping in spangles tonight
> We're working all angles tonight
> Some Bogie, some Lauren
> Some local, some foreign!

April, impressed, yet wondered if Cecil had composed it to prove he was born after the First World War.

By the looks they were getting from others, they exulted in being seen together. Jerry's attraction to April took a jump.

SO, APRIL! he shouted. He caught her eye. ARE YOU UP FOR MY SHOWING YOU WHERE I LIVE AFTER WE LEAVE?

April laughed, brainlessly. Had she even heard what he said? She was flailing herself about the floor, her whirling body as out of control as an unsupervised puppy.

Less than an hour later, out under a silent moon barely visible in the grainy sky, Jerry was walking April up to the front door of his one-bedroom apartment. She, slightly sloshed, seemed amenable to most anything. Inside, she pulled herself into a semi-sober frame of mind.

"You've done a lot with it, baker boy," she said.

"Please, sit anywhere you want, April."

"Anywhere." She viewed the limited options.

"Coffee or tea?"

"Oh, black tea, please. I should sober up."

Jerry went into the kitchen, just as a phone in there was ringing. April sat on the small couch, trying to hear what Jerry was saying to the caller.

"No, I couldn't now .... a friend over ... hanging out ...no, no. Why didn't you? Did call ... you never called back ..."

He sounded irked. April thought girlfriend. He had somebody else. She felt the sting of a rivalry. ".... so let's be ...." Jerry's voice from the other room. "No. Okay, this time, when I call, return my call, alright? ... no, I'm sorry, too!"

Silence.

Presently, Jerry returned with a cup of tea for April, a coffee for himself.

"Some people," he said.

"Some people," she agreed.

"Not even worth talking about." He sat down next to his date, but at a gentlemanly distance.

"That was fun, Jerry," she said, leaning back as if willing to bend a tad the rules of male-to-female friendship.

"You look a little tired, April. You can stay here if you wish."

Where would I sleep, April thought. Those arms of his are strong. I would have to sleep with him. I bet there's only one bed. Jerry placed his hand across her shoulder and caressed it softly.

No, I shouldn't, she was telling herself. Lord, no! Not tonight. Not yet. If I do, tomorrow morning, what? Another tomorrow morning making me ask myself, why? Why, April?

She straightened up, and pushed her dizzy ambivalence off the couch and onto her feet. And glanced down upon Jerry sitting there, looking crestfallen.

"I should be going," she said. "I really should."

"I understand," he replied. Something about his letting go so easily surprised her. He did have somebody else in his life, she feared, the person he was just talking with on the phone, she suspected.

She started to walk across the room, ready to leave. "Thanks, my friend," she said, smiling.

Jerry rose from the couch, completely letting go. April took another secretly admiring look at him, and could not help herself. "That shirt looks good on you."

"You like it?"

"Hot!"

"I just bought it, last week."

"Cotton?"

"A little, maybe...."

Suddenly feeling safe again, April touched Jerry's shirt, ostensibly to sample the texture, but felt a sharp ripple of desire. Jerry noticed the change in her, and clasped her hand, enveloping it in his and softly stroking it.

"So you think it fits me, April?"

Acting tipsy to give herself cover, April sighed. "Perfectly."

He kissed her on the cheek. She wavered. "I'm glad you like it, April."

"Yes, I know you're glad," said April. "I feel dizzy."

"Here, sit down for a second before we leave."

"Yes, before we leave," she agreed, tottering over to the couch, and falling onto it, Jerry joining her, his arms slipping around her backside, and the two giving into whatever next might naturally occur. He longed to take her into his bedroom.

April was losing herself, to him? Or to a drunken stupor? Jerry felt suddenly overcome by a hollowness in their clumsy foreplay. He was on the verge of seducing a woman who wanted them to be friends— when she was sober — and it made him feel like a thief in collusion with alcohol. It was not real. He had not earned it. He pulled back from the careless entanglement, determined to end the evening on a high note.

Jerry's withdrawal startled April. She sat up, too. What had she done wrong?

"I'm sorry," he said. "I got carried away. I think I should take you home, we've had a great night."

"Yes, we have," she agreed, looking around, holding back a burp and pushing her body up off the couch and onto its feet. Jerry assisted.

"Okay, Jerry."

He gave her a long hug. "I'm sorry, April. I think I lost it."

"It's okay. Blame me."

"We're still friends?"

"Yes." Her eyes opened wide.

"Good. I don't want to lose you."

How flattering of him, she thought, still feeling rejected. Something I did. Something he felt. He was all over me. I gave in too easily. She knew she'd maybe had too much to drink, but not that much, really. She had used it, shamelessly, as a pretense for her loose behavior.

Jerry sounded so formal. "I had a great time, April."

They were walking out the front door, onto the sidewalk.

"I did too," she agreed. Any man, given the chance I gave him, would have taken me to bed. Would have ripped my clothes to shreds and had at me. What went wrong? God, is he homo? All those passes, what for? Too fat! The donuts, what for? Who are we? He could have taken advantage. He didn't. He controlled himself. Okay, he respects me, April! So don't' go crazy analyzing it down the drain.

They got into the car. Jerry drove April back to Encore. On the way, April complimented Jerry on his dancing. He raved about hers. They talked about the people at the club, and they laughed. They talked about April's first new tenant. About the warm evening weather. The smog. The sun. Jerry's job.

Jerry stopped the car in front of Encore, leaned over to give April a kiss.

"I enjoyed it just as much you did, Jerry," she said, getting out, waving back and going up the steps.

Jerry drove off, thinking about the phone call he had taken while she was at his place, and feeling less a hypocrite. Wishing, still, that April felt as happy as he did.

## CHAPTER 8

Came a big Saturday for Tiffany, the first morning in her new apartment. The sun was out with a blast, but she was stuck inside, waiting on the phone company to install her telephone. Finally, a man arrived, around 10:30, and, in less than ten minutes, her service was restored. Now, when Troy tried reaching her, he would be given her this number by the recorded voice.

She felt so good and hopeful, reconnected to the world, and decided to take a little exploratory walk around her new neighborhood. Upon returning, the message machine's red light was ablaze. Three messages! Anxiously, she picked up to replay them. She thrilled to the voice on the first left message.

"Ah, Tiffany?"

It was him. Her leaped

Street sounds. Other voices cluttering up the background. And then? Where was he now? She held the receiver tight to her ear:

"Prick!"

"How much"

"Off my ass!"

The connection died.

She pressed the button to message number two.

"Tiffany?"

Troy again!

But then silence. Nothing. He's afraid, she sensed.

A hang-up.

"Message number three..."

"So much like a poem burning over asphalt ... so much, like ... what? No, hold on, okay?'

A hang-up. And silence.

"You have no more messages."

The evidence of his being in town was all she needed at this point. She skated around the room without skates, made love without him being there, danced into the bathroom to self deceivingly admire her winning face in the non-committal mirror. To see why Troy had been unable to let go. They were fated!

Her predatory eyes surveyed the unmake bed. Now, it had meaning. She would not lift it back into wall. She would keep it down, for convenience. Too difficult to put back every day, she would tell him. She pictured him, late nights, walking around it with his shirt open, his jeans loose and slipping below his waistline, sitting down and looking up at her, and slowly surrendering.

She walked over to the window, and looked down. The stranger was not there.

Troy was not a stalker. Troy would face you in person. Troy is an artist like I am an artist, she told herself. He understands me like few do.

She sat down upon the bed like a smitten school girl, laid back and stretched out into a long tunnel waiting to be traveled. This time he would travel her all the way through.

It would not be long now. And then, it would be very long.

The next morning, a Sunday not yet fully in bloom, April was sitting in her kitchen and nursing the fear of another rejection that had followed so many one-night stands. She looked out the window to a partial sun, more than half of it stalled behind a band of deadbeat clouds. She took refuge in her tea, and tried to shake off yesterday's blues. She was bothered by Jerry's having not given her a pink box after he had driven her home from the night club, as he had promised. Bothered enough to turn the snub into a three-act tragedy featuring him and some other woman, not April. Had it been in reaction to her abandon on his couch? Had she not provoked it?

Her mind was a traffic jam of conspiracy theories blaming the unsettling outcome of their date on many things — from the color of the new blouse she had bought for the occasion, to a tiny patch of unshaven hair under her left armpit. To the painfully unthinkable: Her weight. If ever she wanted to write to Dear Abby. But how could she ever put this all in words? Abby did not take trial briefs.

Tiffany had lunch on Sunday afternoon with Steven at the old fashioned Yellow House on Melrose. She had never seen him quite so happy. His date with Gary the night before had gone like a dream. They spent the night together, and talked about things they would like to do.

"It felt like we were starting all over again," he sighed.

"So, what happened to him and the other fellow?"

"He didn't say much. I don't think they had been seeing each other very long. He seemed a little uneasy to talk about it."

And Tiffany was made to feel uneasy about whatever might still be going on between Gary and the other fellow, but she kept her reservations to herself, happy to see Steve in such high spirits.

Upon returning to her new studio, Tiffany, hoping so much for the same kind of a reunion with Troy, hurried over to the message machine. Red light off. Rejection in the air. She made herself some coffee, sat down in the armchair, restless for something to do, but unable to do much of anything. She listened to the phone not ringing. She went through a box of manuscripts, pulled out the first draft of a screenplay that she had been laboring over for many years, and tried reading it just to occupy herself. After ten pages, she felt depressingly detached from her own writing.

She went downstairs and out the front door. The warm early evening enfolded her in an empty calm. In this town, an empty calm could make loneliness feel almost secondary. She walked around the block, and then walked back into Encore Apartments, up the stairs to her unit, went inside and looked at the answering machine to find the red light unlit. Discouraged and distressed, she lay down on the bed, waiting. It was only nine o'clock. Too early for sleep.

Now was the time he was inclined to call. Now or even later. She could wait all night.

Close to midnight, Tiffany was roused from a light sleep by the phone's ringing. She jostled out of bed, and hurried to answer it, but then held back. Now, she felt submerged in darkness. Now she was again ensnared in the senseless shackles of lust. Now was the witching hour. Desperation. Was this the emotion to be feeling the second time around? Was this even the time when they should give a second time a chance? The emotion and the question tied her in knots, and she stood there in a freeze, listening to her own words while fearing what his might be.

"Please leave your message after the beep."

Beep.

"Hi, ah, Tiffany. I hope this is your phone."

It was him. She wanted to pick up, but couldn't. Something about the rough voices she had heard in the background during his first call. She stood in a frozen limbo, casting judgement while he spoke:

"I'm here in hooray for Hollywood. Yeah, surprise! Came out to see the town for myself, maybe compose some. I see you moved." He broke away, distracted by somebody else. To the other person, "What? No, that's not me. Hey!" Voices in a scuffle. A car's honking. The connection died.

She felt relieved, liberated, excited, too. He'll call back, she told herself. When she could not have him, she wanted him. And when she could have him, she could become afraid. What now? Was he in a fight? Down to his last penny? He needs me. I should have answered. Why didn't I? He'll think I am avoiding him. Might not call back. Where is he? She went back to bed, but, unable to sleep, lay there in the gloom, facing another empty night fraught with such infantile desire. And she felt shallow. And yet she lay there hoping the phone would ring, knowing she might not answer it but draw solace from his hovering presence.

On Monday morning, the next day, Tiffany, soon after showing up for work at the private eye's office on Hollywood, near Western, was told by the boss to take the day off, with pay. He had just been dumped by the new client he had expected to entertain that morning, and was now going to spend the day on a golf course, entertaining another prospective client burdened by, as her boss would short hand it, "MFS," for "malfunctioning spouse."

So, Tiffany, relieved, went down onto the street, to catch a bus home. She spotted a long limbo driving by, and in the back seat— her eyes nearly flying out of their sockets—*Troy*? She wanted to run after the car, but then came to her senses. She had often spotted other young men who looked like Troy. The farther away she was from the sighting, the easier it was to fool herself. No, let it go. Standing at the bus stop, and waiting, she noticed the same car, or so it appeared, coming her way. But the figure of Troy, if that's who it was, was now missing.

Later that morning at Encore, Manny was gunning up the old Buick, which he had washed down and polished up on Sunday, for a ride up the Reseda with April. They breezed through Hollywood without showing off, and passed Capital records on Vine, where Manny had once worked, managing the charts. Manny's mint-condition 1948 cream orange Buick Super Convertible carried them efficiently over the Cahuenga pass. At Sherman Way, Manny turned left.

The wide street ahead felt both intimate and alien, as so much of Los Angeles did to people from other places. A nasty layer of morning smog was promising a day of balmy suppression. Here was where the eternal heat of Los Angeles came to a suffocating climax. Where people with breathing problems and wishing to make a career of them settled. People hunkered down inside their fine homes, fanned by air conditioners, or they swam in backyard pools. Rows and rows of prosperous-looking middle class homes, punctuated by corner shopping malls and the occasional church or massage parlor, spelled the American good life — if only the air quality would cooperate.

"How are you and the baker boy getting on"

April shrunk in her seat.

"What's wrong?"

"The other night," she answered. She leveled with Manny on what had happened at Jerry's apartment after the club, and Manny turned philosophical:

"Give it some time, April. Your parents didn't give you your name for nothing."

April laughed. "So April waits for May ... for September?"

"Good things take time. Two people meet, they're a mystery to each other. And even if they stick it out, they're still mysteries."

"Was your wife a mystery?"

"Oh, she could be. That part I left alone. You can't have therapy in the home. If you let it in, love walks out."

Manny let up on the pedal as the traffic lights turned against him. They had reached Sherman Way and Reseda Boulevard.

"We're only about a block away."

April warmed to a familiar sight on the other side. "My old skating rink! Open already?"

"This early in the morning?"

"Must be a private party."

Manny reminisced. "I used to skate in Melbourne."

"Oh, my God," said April, "Melissa? Is that her?"

"Where?"

"In the parking lot by the rink. Look She's on skates! In a bikini!"

Manny spotted the figure. "My Lord, our own Marilyn Monroe on ball bearings?" He chuckled.

April reported, "She's rolling inside. What is going on in there?"

"An adults-only affair?"

"Are you kidding? In a roller rink. I wonder if it was her."

The lights turned green, and Manny drove on. "We could go in, maybe after checking out Dreamland Productions, and see."

"Wouldn't that be fun." .

Manny squeezed the car between a BMW and a flatbed.

"Back in Melbourne, I used to roll around rinks a lot. I was a pretty fair dancer on wheels."

"Did they have a Victorian bunny hop?"

They cracked each other up.

"I took a few lessons," said April, "got as far as the Chase Waltz and, what was the other one? The Southland Swing."

"Oh, I did the Southland Swing," said Manny.

They got out and walked up the street in search of 18553,

posted on the edge of a building with an arrow pointing to an alley that led to an aging, narrow staircase.

"This must be it," he said.

"So, should I go up first?"

"Yeah. My presence might put them off. You're here for an audition, fresh in from — from where?"

"Glendale?"

Manny laughed. "Make up a place, far away. You've got big dreams of being in movies."

"That's who I am."

"Let them play their hand. Just don't sign anything. I'll be waiting in the car." He hurried off.

April headed up the rickety staircase. At the top, she faced a door, and tired pushing it to see if it would open, when it opened itself. Out came a short squat man with a fat cigar to match.

"Here for an audition?"

"Yes," she said, breathlessly, stifling the urge to giggle.

"You know it's an adult film?"

"Ah, yes."

The man looked her over. "A little too ... maybe for a crowd scene, I think you'll do. Street clothing. You've got a good face."

How April liked hearing that.

He told her to go to the skating rink down the street. "Tell them at the door that Freddie told you to ask for Goodwin."

"Freddie to Goodwin?"

"That's it."

He slipped back behind the door, April hurried down to Manny's car, to tell him she'd been hired. "Sounds like porno. They're using some people in street clothes. I want to peek inside, to see what I can find. Won't be long!"

"Take your time. I've no pressing matters," said Many, and she hurried off. He was remembering the night when he took the woman who would be his wife skating. Only their second date. His fancy dancing on rollers had impressed her.

Inside, the rink was swarming with skaters of all sizes, a few of them fat. A few of them skinny. Some downright ugly. *Am I supposed to be a fat woman,* wondered April. *Is this some kind of an all-God's children got sex appeal movie?* And she laughed.

Skaters glided through pockets of darkness. The center seemed reserved for the stars on wheels. Most of them were wearing mostly their skin. Horny-looking cameras were rolling on a platform that skated through the crowd, like in a Fellini flick. How impressive! April seemed to remember that Fellini liked heavy set women. There were a few of them rolling by on skates, but the sight of them flailing about like wild Italian whores made April sick to her stomach. Is this what they have in mind for me? She felt nauseous.

And where was Melissa? April could not find her anywhere. The crowd became intense, and April started feeling dizzy in the midst of it all. Blasting disco music was loud enough to demolish the building. She found a bench, and sat down, needing to regroup and take a few deep breaths.

'Hey, girl, where are your skates?' shouted a man in the crowd.

"Oh, I was just watching."

She got up, and tried standing still for a moment, and felt okay and headed for the front door, and hurried out, feeling liberated from a communal orgy, feeling a desire to take in a Sunday service at Aime Semple McPherson's Four Square Gospel Temple at Echo Park and have the stench of all of this washed away.

Back inside Manny's Buick, she amused him with the scurrilous details.

He gunned up the motor.

"Back to the Bible Belt?" he asked.

April cracked, "I never thought of Hollywood as the Bible Belt!"

"All things are relative."

"Right you are, sir."

They chortled merrily on.

The old Buick groaned for a stretch, and then purred over the Cahuenga pass, as if happy to be returning to the town where it could count on a little respect.

"The ladies loved skating with Manny," reminisced Manny. "Never sat out a couples-only or a ladies choice!"

April thought how much fun it would be to go skating with Manny. Maybe he could join her and Jerry for a night at the rink.

And there he was, ruling her thoughts again—Jerry. She thought pink box. Another pang pierced her heart. Would she ever even see him again? She was hurting, she had to admit to herself. Maybe he was not exactly her type, but he had so many better things to offer her than most of the clods she usually chased, or was chased by.

That Monday afternoon, Troy was downstairs at a pay phone in the dingy lobby of an ancient building that looked only a few urban renewal votes away from demolition. It stood in semi-secrecy, a block north of Hollywood Boulevard, the street barely a street at all, more like an alley that led to nowhere in a section of town that had once, no doubt, thrived with motion picture people and aspiring starry-eyed newcomers, some of them playing the role of hangers-on for gainful employment, by day scrubbing bathtubs and fetching junk food on a tray for the sainted one up there in bed, and telling callers at the door that the sainted one was not at the moment in.

The old barn looked strong enough and stubborn enough to survive any act of God, if not defy it entirely. This was where Troy's new friend off the streets, Rusty, lived, compliments of the absentee "producer" who rented space on the third floor — dubbed by old timers in days gone by "the jumping off floor" — to use for X-rated "cinema." The producer would amuse young star-struck actors after being told what was really up at this studio. You wanted MGM? We can offer you S&M?"

Troy had tried reaching Tiffany at her new phone number. It rang and rang without the message machine clicking on. He took it as a snub, and had an easier time thinking about calling up the mysterious once-was star up in the Valley. Grab the money while it's there. Three hundred dollars and he had done virtually nothing. But, dare he risk setting off one of her beefy boyfriends? He went back to Rusty's apartment, where breakfast was waiting for him.

"Your eggs, Troy?"

"Oh, surprise me," answered Troy, thinking of offering to treat Rusty to a movie up the street.

# CHAPTER 9

Came Monday's early evening, and Steven was standing outside the door to Tiffany's new apartment.

Moments later, it opened.

"Steven!"

"How was your day, Tiff? Better than mine, I hope."

"I got most of the day off, with pay. Boss was stood up by one client, and went off to golf with another."

She motioned him to come inside.

"So, one for the boss," said Steve, dropping into a chair at the little round table. The bed had been raised. Tiffany noticed shadows of hurt across his face.

"Now, what is it, Steve?"

He shook his head in disbelief. "I can't believe it."

"You and ... Gary?"

"Yes, he ... Gary."

"So, what happened?"

"Last night he called, sounding excited, and we talked for a long time. Now, I could feel, he was coming around to my way. Finally, he would agree to a monogamous relationship, and so he was coming back to offer it to me. I don't want to spend the rest of my life in the bars, I really don't. Or going out with a so-called lover to pick up men to share."

"I know you don't."

"I would like to have somebody to come home to, somebody who is there. Not on some of the nights, maybe, but on all of them."

"I understand. And so?"

"Maybe he forgot all about the reason why we split up in the first place. Or maybe he was..."—Steve took a pause—"just horny. So, one hot night together back under the sheets together is what he really wanted."

"So, is that such a bad thing? He might want to get back together."

"Sure, he wants what he had before."

"Then, did you ask him about a serious relationship."

"Serious? You mean open?"

Tiffany did not answer the question.

"He still thinks we should be able to see others. He promised not to be as promiscuous now as he was before."

"That's a start."

"He is still seeing the fellow he supposedly broke up with. Nothing has changed."

Steve erupted into anger and tears. "I feel like I've been played with. I'm just another easy lay in his life!"

"You poor thing," said Tiffany, coming over to put her arms around him, and run them down his front side in a motherly embrace. "Being in love takes courage."

"Being in lust does too," he said, laughing away the hurt, and feeling a rise. "I know, I know. Don't say it. Monogamy is a pipe dream."

"Still, I think you should give Gary a second chance. Maybe he'll come around in time."

"By the time we're both in a nursing home? No, it's me who will have to come around."

"At least see how it works, no?"

She touched his shoulder lovingly, feeling freer to advance, given Gary's casual attitudes.

"I'm not sure. I almost feel like I was set up. Like a crushed little boy with a broken toy on Christmas morning. The toy I dreamed all year of getting."

"Well, this little boy is going to get over it," she said, stroking Steve's hair.

"That feels good," he sighed.

"Just relax and let go, Steve."

He sat there, passively transfixed.

"Close your eyes."

He closed his eyes.

She moved one hand down over his chest, and started to massage him sensually.

Suddenly surprised, he felt himself the object of her desire. He sat up and away, and she let go. "I'm fooling myself again, I know," he confessed. "How easy it is to have an open relationship. To whore around all night and still have somebody to come home to — that is, on the nights when they come home."

"I don't think most men are wired for what you want. You might not be yourself. There's a lovely fellow down the hall. Maybe he is."

Steve felt the promise of sexual escape, wondering who she might be talking about.

"He broke up with his lover recently, I hear. He's still hoping they'll get back together."

Steve found himself hoping he wouldn't, wanting to believe that Tiffany had been talking about the striking fellow he had passed coming up the stairs.

A light tap tap tap on the door. Tiffany went over to open it. Manny was standing there, next to a small table with two pull-out drawers.

"Think this might do for a typing stand, Tiffany?"

"Oh, it's wonderful ! Please do bring it in."

"Here," said Steve, springing to his feet. "Let me help."

He and Manny exchanged friendly nods, and they carried the desk into the room.

"By the window would be perfect."

"By the window it shall be," said Manny.

"Looks great," said Steve, crossing to the door, his spirit revived. "Got to go, Tiff. I'll call you later. Thanks for everything. Cheers, Manny!"

"Same to you!"

Steven was out the door and down the hall at a slower gait, wondering where the man Tiffany had in mind for him lived. On this floor. He wanted to linger, but reigned in his shallow side, and kept walking.

Back in Tiffany's place, she was sitting at the little table Manny had brought her, and he was standing over her, enjoying the view.

"It's a keeper, Manny!"

"It fits in right well."

"I already feel reborn. The perfect place to write in the morning!"

"We had a fellow in here, some years back, he liked this space, same as you. Funny fellow, another Hemingway would-be, he was writing a novel called 'For Whom the Toilets Flush.'"

Tiffany laughed her head off.

Manny chuckled. "Some of the characters we get. You'll find plenty of material around here."

Not wishing to overstay, he crossed to the door to leave.

"Thank you, Manny!"

"Enjoy chapter one!" He paused. "Who knows, it may be staring at you from out the window!"

And he left. Tiffany Orr sat down at her new desk, pondering Manny's parting remark. She sampled pulling out the drawers. She looked out the window, down below. Nobody.

The telephone rang.

She rushed to answer it, but held back.

Was it Troy, she hoped, her heart on fire. She stood there frozen in fear. She picked up. Hello? She waited in silence. Said hello again. Waited. Was it him? No street sounds or background voices. A good omen. Must be Troy, still afraid to take a first step. She could wait. A knock on the door. Maybe she didn't have to. Him? But how would he know where she lived, unless Steve had given him her address?

She put the telephone back and went over to the door, and looked through the peephole: there stood her new neighbor whom, somebody had told her, was stuck on old movie musicals. Feeling not one drop of desire, she had no fear of opening it for this visitor.

"And a great good evening to you!" said Cecil Fanton.

April felt as if she were being announced on stage to receive a Lifetime Achievement Award.

"And a great good evening yourself!"

"We've not formally met, I don't think," he offered.

"Not even informally. You are, Cecil?"

"Cecil. Yes."

"I remember you from the other day, and thanks for offering to help with my move in."

"Did it go all right?"

"I have so few possessions, it was like bringing groceries home."

Just then, the door directly across the hall flung open, admitting Wayne into the hall, who glanced at Tiffany for the first time, not without passing interest, and went down to the end of the corridor and down the stairs.

Cecil spoke in deep austere tones. "Have you met him?"

"No, I haven't.'

"A little edgy. He and his girlfriend can be loud. Management's not happy."

"They aren't?"

"Between you and me, I hear the building owner wants those two out."

"Really?"

"But, what about you. Somebody told me you write screenplays?"

"I do, I do!" she sang, cheered by his interest. "Still waiting for a break."

"Aren't we all," said Cecil. "A tough business. I'm on the Hollywood fringe myself, my forte being golden age musicals."

"New ones?"

"Oh, yes, originals! I just finished a new song, buzzing in my brain, I can see it bringing down the house. This will put MGM back on the map."

"What's it called?"

"Grabbing the Great White Way."

"I like it! And, how rude of me not to invite you in. Please, do!"

She opened the door wider, and Cecil came inside. "Thank you."

"You're most welcome. Do have a chair. Either one!"

Cecil sat down at the table. "I wrote my new musical with Pearl Dubuque in mind."

"Pearl Dubuque?"

"The woman down the hall, a legend in her time."

"Dubuque?"

"No, you've probably never heard the name. Gloria Swanson got all the press. There were two or three others just as good."

"I don't know much about that," said Tiffany, amused by his child-like faith in old musicals from a bygone era.

Cecil Fanton was in his element defending long forgotten icons. "Can I try it out on you? The song?"

"Of course! I'm all ears! Sing for me!"

"I like testing my new tunes just like Irving Berlin did, on anybody out there at the moment willing to give them an ear."

"Well," said Tiffany. "Try your song on mine. They're open!"

The budding songwriter rose from his chair and assumed the brisk posture of a $42^{nd}$ Street hoofer, circa 1930. He moved a little awkwardly, as if he been taught to dance through correspondence instruction. His barreling voice gave off a certain timbre that sounded like it came with an operating saw mill.

Tap tap tap tap, snap your fingers and shine
Grab grab grab grab, make that next audition be mine!
Grabbing the great white way, let go of your bitching!
Grabbing the great white way, you gotta go pitching!

Cecil was getting caught up in the song, and Tiffany lost herself in his bombastic delivery. At least, it gave her a respite from obsessing over Troy. And the two had fun fooling each other.

"Bravo!" sang Tiffany Orr, one of whose enduring gifts was offering generous praise to others for their creative efforts, however rudimentary. Cecil was overjoyed. What a wonderful new neighbor, and right next door!

Downstairs at April's place about an hour later, Manny was sitting at the table sipping tea, looking perfectly relaxed and open to whatever train of thought might rattle through his brain. He and April had been talking about the Melissa Cusp matter, considering how they might mount damaging evidence to suggest that she was doing actual adult film work in her apartment.

Grounds for eviction.

The doorbell rang. April opened it. Cecil stood behind a staged smile, beaming at the woman he could see putting over his torch song for Grabbing the Great White Way, "Broadway Blues."

"Hello, Cecil. Come in!"

"You are a true lady," said Cecil, entering and spotting Manny. "I have been wanting to ask you about Pearl Dubuque."

There it is, thought Manny. Cecil proceeded to argue his case for meeting the elusive lady upstairs. She would be perfect for his all-singing all-dancing movie. Manny remembered his Squaw Man, the Musical crack to April, but kept it to himself. He sat there and patiently listened, charmed, and agreed to see if he could find a way to pigeon-hole Cecil through into the gothic cave of Dubuque.

On Tuesday, after taking her lunch at a Mexican grill next to the Pantages Theater on Hollywood and Vine, Tiffany was walking back to work when a passing white 1960 Lincoln Continental bore a young male figure in the back seat who looked like, could it be him — *him*. Again? Her heart went wild. Troy, being chauffeured across town? Of course; he had the looks. Her footsteps lunged after the Lincoln. She prayed for traffic jams to slow down its steady advance. Half a block up, she watched it turn left. She nearly ran up the street to see where, once it turned, it might be headed, or parked. She came upon a narrow alley that led to a dead end that looked dark and shunted aside. She could not spot the car. Must have lost it. Drats!

How she longed to keep walking in abstract pursuit. If it were him and the two accidentally met, what might he think? Hell, she rationalized, I could say I was out for a lunch walk and I saw you.

She reigned in her gait and proceeded casually, coming upon a cul-de-sac of haphazardly parked cars and a few still-lingering old trees refusing to expire. The Lincoln Continental came back into the scene, moving slowly in her direction, apparently on its way out. She snapped a quick look of the riders, and could only spot the driver, a paunchy middle-aged man of worn looks with a cigarette dangling off his lower lip, who looked like he lived on remote control. She glanced back as the Lincoln reached the street and made a right turn.

At the end of the alley stood an old stone building, maybe four stories high. Did anybody live there? Conduct business in there? It looked forlorn, a still standing albatross from another age having escaped urban renewal. Some of the windows were missing glass. A few of them had frayed curtains or white sheets keeping out the sun. Most of them like the empty eyes of an architectural death. Upon the sills of some, birds perched. But the building stood tall and stubborn — like a lumbering giant refusing to die, daring the world to try to tear it down. It must be a magnet, she assumed, for the homeless.

If that had been Troy in the car, he might be living here. Or knows somebody who does. It made sense. He, like she, thrived on the tough fringes of society, and this place, if it still contained human life in any form, was about as far on the edge as one could get.

She walked up to the front door, into a dreary, dusty alcove, feeling a strange erotic connection to Troy. Whatever might be going on inside this morose mausoleum? On a wall there were little mail boxes, rusting away. Some bore names of occupants on white strips of card stock. Some were opened; some no longer had doors on them.

She pressed her face close to the thick, heavily stained glass on one of the two front doors, and strained to make out the interior, barely visible through the shadows. The lobby looked dirty, disfigured, ignored. She saw a staircase, as roughly defined as a pencil sketch. Did people actually live here? Did they climb those wobbly-looking steps? She felt poetically moved by the bleakness.

Thundering down the stairs came a heavy male figure, who hit the ground running. Tiffany retreated to the side of the door, and out through it he heaved himself, scampering wildly up the alley to the street. Tiffany froze in a fear for Troy, wondering if he was inside and had anything to do with this.

She pushed against the doors to go inside, and somebody else came rushing down the steps. She watched a tall rangy kid of maybe twenty, shirtless, with a shock of dirty blond hair, holding a skate board in his right hand. He darted out onto the wavy cement, flipped his board laterally into action, flung himself onto it, and rode it up the alley and out onto the boulevard.

She looked around in perverse curiosity, feeling like she had reached an outpost at the edge of western civilization. She heard angry voices from above. And then — a gunshot? She went back outside and pretended to be looking for somebody among the names on the mail boxes that had names ... A. J. Lindler Investigations.... Stars Unlimited ... Script Clinic .... Ground Zero Films ... Take-A-Chance Productions. Some were aging and crinkled, others half torn and peeling away.

Out through the door stumbled a chunky man with one hand covering a bloody nose, running up the alley to the street and disappearing from view.

Tiffany stood there transfixed. Maybe Troy was not here, but somewhere else, she hoped. Anywhere but here. Maybe somewhere up the narrow alley on the near side of the building. She wanted to let go. Is this all I am? All I will ever be? Traipsing back and forth between dumps like this, between restless young men destined to go nowhere in life? Tennessee Williams, he was like that, wasn't he? He would understand me, how my life goes from one failed scene to another. I am a play by Tennessee Williams.

A man wearing security attire came up. "You're looking for somebody, Miss?"

"No, I was wondering if they rent."

"Rent." He chuckled. "This place. Yeah, they rent, to a lot of characters you would not want to meet."

"Really?"

"Unless you're one of them." He stifled a cheap laugh. "If you're not looking to be in a horror film, or one of the adult jobs, I'd stay clear of the place."

He went inside.

Tiffany returned to her office job, stabilizing her anxieties with happier thoughts of Steven, wanting to introduce him to Jared, whom, from what she had learned, might be the more faithful tupe.

Wednesday morning felt unusually depressing to April. She wondered how Cecil might set her feeling to a song. Every day that passed without a call from Jerry only drove her depression deeper. Were they history? He had been calling her at least every other day — and that all stopped following their aborted

North Hollywood tryst five days ago. Nothing since. Why had she made such a fool of herself? He saw the wrong me, her monitoring voice screamed. Why did I let him? Yes, why did you, it shouted back. Oh, God, now he sees me as easy. He's the one in control. Why am I even thinking this way? We are supposed to be FRIENDS. Hold that thought! shouted her interior voice. Yes, I'm clinging to it, promise, she answered.

Sitting there over an empty tea cup in despair, sitting there feeling too hopeless to get up and boil more water, April tried to cry. There were no more tears left. If only she could release all the pain inside. If only it would go away.

She got up, resolved to do something. She could make her morning tour of the premises.

She opened the door, and down in front of it stood a pink box.

Glory to God, sang April and her monitoring voices in chorus. Never again, we promise!

She took the box inside and opened it up. Never had it meant so much. There were plain old fashions and a few butter croissants.

A note inside read, "So, I'm trying to be a better friend, April. Hope these little selections satisfy your sweet tooth without making you feel guilty! Loving Cheers, Jerry."

Tears of joy caressed her round rosy cheeks.

The telephone rang. She took the call.

"April." Jerry's voice.

"Hi, Jerry, and thanks for the goodies! I just found them at the door."

"Perfect timing. Dropped them off on my way to work."

"That's right. You start early."

"That I do," he said. "I thought you might welcome a change of calorie intake."

"You read my mind perfectly."

"Lots of news," Jerry announced, shifting subjects. "Haven't too much time. I'm on a break. Had my hair re-styled yesterday. It cost me twenty-nine bucks."

"You spent twenty=nine dollars on your hair?"

"Let's say that I was inspired by someone, which brings me to the other good news."

Was he about to ask her out again?

"My ears are as big as an elephant's," she said.
"I think I'm falling in love."
April crashed. It doesn't sound like me, she feared.
"You are?" she said, ferociously holding a forced composure, while a voice from within mocked her with a teasing giggle -- just friends, April! Remember?
"Somebody I met a while back," he revealed.
What a cruel thing to do, thought April. He brings me donuts and tells me about a new crush? She wanted to scream, but was able to restrain herself. She would have to settle for merely feeling romantically rejected. This would not have to mean they were done.
"I have so much to tell you, April. Are you free this evening?"
April felt resentful, and close to losing it, but contained her agitation.
Jerry explained, "I need to talk to somebody. And you, you are my dearest friend still — I hope."
That cheered her a bit. "Dearest" would have to suffice for now. I'd better play the role, she decided.
"Dearest," repeated April. "How quaint. Should I wear a bonnet?"
Jerry howled. "Very funny, April! So, can I drop by your place, say around five thirty, and we can go somewhere, get a bite to eat, and talk."
In her jealousy, she felt like the other woman, and, strange, the unwelcome thought actually made it seem as if they had drawn closer.
"Okay, Jerry. Sure. I'll be here."
"Great! Gotta get back to the ovens. See you later."
He hung up.
April turned to Jerry's latest gesture of affection — plain old fashioneds in a charity box. Take one. Take two. Take them all, she thought. I deserve something! She talked herself into believing there were ulterior motives in Jerry's wanting to speak with her about a new love interest. Probably to make me jealous. The notion calmed her nerves. Yes. Okay, I'll be the perfect model of friendship. And I had better, while I am at it, make us equal by telling him my own good news about the Englishman I met up at the equestrian center. Good news was an overstatement,

but April needed equity to carry on the friendship charade. That should balance things out quite nicely.

Under a flashing setting sun later in the dry day, April was faking gladness for Jerry's new romance, the two relaxing over the grass back of the tar pits by the county art museum. They were enjoying Kentucky Fried Chicken dinners they had picked up along the way. The darkening spring evening, as warm as an electric blanket, kept April's nascent envy in check. Yes, no, no, he is a friend. We are friends. Make the most of this; at least, he hasn't thrown me over. Be grateful, April, and may May be better. How like a Cecil Fanton song it sounded. She thought of sharing the idea with her new suitor upstairs. *Cecil, a new flame?!*

She heard Jerry's voice, and lurched back into the role of a listening buddy. "She seems really into me." he was saying. "When I called her the next night, we talked for over two hours."

April sighed, pretending to share. "Those long calls can feel like a dream."

"And we went out to the Santa Monica boardwalk on Sunday."

"How lovely," she lied.

"She likes the beach," he said.

He'll never see me in a swimsuit, April vowed.

"We're going out again this next week," he said.

"I hope they drown in the ocean," she wished.

"Thus, my new hairdo, ta da!"

April looked at Jerry's stylish new top, a little overdone to her eyes, but smiled.

"Do you like it?" he asked.

"I do," she answered. "Cool, yes."

"I wanted to see what you thought," he said. "Oh, and," he remembered. "She likes to go camping."

"And, do you, Jerry? You never said anything to me about camping?"

"I used to go camping with the Boy Scouts. I liked it, yes."

April did not believe that he liked it. One point for her side.

"So, she's the outdoor type?"

"She likes the water. Her father owns a yacht."

"Impressive, "granted April in another lie, wondering if Jerry were the gold-digger in this affair. "It feels natural. We are both so into each other."

Sure, April thought. I'll give them, max, two trips to the bedroom.

"What's her name, Jerry?"

"Oh yes. Misha."

"Misha. Sounds Russian."

"She is. Came to the States last year."

"Green card, green card to deportation," April hoped.

"She called me up last night," he sighed, the first sign of trouble. "She wants to go Catalina Island for a weekend. Maybe July fourth."

"And?"

"She has her heart set on a certain hotel. The rates are not low."

"Like, what is not low?" asked April.

"How about two hundred a night."

"Are you splitting the cost?"

Jerry balked. "I'm not sure."

"You'd better be." April hoped he landed a greedy Russian, knowing how good the odds were that he would be taken on a one-way ride to dumpsville.

Jerry gauged April's odd reaction. "So what are you thinking?"

April gathered her thoughts, the monitor within glaring at her. Yes, she answered back, I am his friend in this moment. So be his friend, damn it! She could be quite hard on herself.

Her counsel to Jerry: "Well, unless she's willing to pay half, why don't you suggest something else. See how she reacts to that, Jerry?"

"I think I should. Good idea."

"So," said April, continuing to admire Jerry's new hair style, "was it her idea?"

He grinned. "How did you guess?"

"She speaks her mind."

Don't be another Misha, April told herself.

"I don't want to lose her. I would like to go to Catalina."

"At what price," asked April, coming alive.

"Good point."

"You need to hold your ground. Tell her it's too much money. Because it is! If she's for real, she will understand.

It's not as if you were a lawyer or doctor with a bank account to match."

"Yes, you're right."

"You're the baker boy, and you have more than mere money to offer."

"Oh, how sweet, April."

The glow in his eyes quickened April's pulse. Maybe Manny was right about the two.

She poured it on. "You've got donuts, plain old fashioned at that!"

They shared a warm laugh.

Rising to the heights of loving advice, April urged caution. She could almost hear Manny coaching her. "Isn't it better to find out who she really is now, rather than waste a lot of time on the wrong person, and suffer later?"

She could feel Jerry's relief. "I knew I should talk to you, April. I think, I'm going to call her tonight."

"Just tell her you like the idea, but you hope she can agree on something less expensive."

"Yes. Yes."

"And feel good about yourself, Jerry. You are a classy guy. I know that now."

How his eyes shone. And how they gave April faith in their date. A nibble upon which to float for a heavenly spell. Wordlessly, they shared a good feeling for not having gone any farther than they did at Jerry's place the other night. Jerry leaned forward, closer. "Thanks for talking. I know I can trust you."

They finished their chicken meal on the grass. Jerry drove April back to Encore, let her out, and returned to his apartment, resolved to call his Russia princess and see if she had some sympathy for a humble baker.

In the early evening, Troy found a pay phone inside the post office on Selma Avenue. He dialed Tiffany's number, hoping, at last, to break the ice.

"Hi, it's Tiffany. Please leave a message so that I can return your call. Cheers, everyone!" Troy waited for the beep.

"Tiffany, hey, guess who this is? Yeah, Troy. I'm in town, thought I'd try the Hollywood scene. So far, so crazy, but I'm holding on. Tried finding you at your old address, and somebody gave me your number. Don't know if you received the letter I sent, hope you did, hope the writing is going good out here. No new poems lately. Only a few lines wandering inside my head."

He wavered over whether or not to give out Rusty's phone number.

"I'm staying with a friend in Hollywood, a place to crash until, well, I'll see how it works out here. You know about these things." Indeed, she did, and what would she think if she called and the wrong person answered? No, Troy decided.

"Ah, what a place. So this is Tinsel Town. People aren't so shallow. Maybe it's the sun. I'll try reaching you later."

While Troy had been talking to Tiffany's answering machine, she had been standing directly over it, ambivalently shaking inside, feeling a womanly score, but fearing a repeat of something too painful to recall. If only she could drive that horrible night out of her brain, banish it forever, as if it had never happened. She felt a competing desire to let go of Troy, while she still had a chance. She had others in her life now — Steven and Cecil, and Manny, and April. Real people. Were they not enough? She let the message play out to the end, and then deleted it, feeling something closer to being able to accept her age.

A knock on her door. Him already? She trembled all over, afraid to answer it, but drawn to a power she had a hard time controlling. And she felt sorry for him, wondering how he was getting on out there in this bag shallow town. And feeling a maternal sympathy. Yes, Tiffany Orr could justify their friendship on these grounds alone. She crossed to the door, and peered through the hole. Another Troy? The hunky fellow from across the hall, whom she had talked to in passing the day before, was out there. He was from New Jersey, he told her, and so, of course, Tiffany's New York just across the Hudson could relate to his Jersey. He had mentioned a sore shoulder that was bothering him and she had mentioned a holistic approach to physical well-being, which included massage. Might this be on his mind? She could not bring herself to open the door. She stood there in limbo, paralyzed in a numbing sense that she was being stalked by the same person, over and over again.

## CHAPTER 10

Around the same time, about forty-five minutes later, Manny was returning from Ralph's supermarket with two arms full of groceries for the screen queen in her dormant hive upstairs. He had stepped into her apartment, briefly, to take them into the kitchen and listen to her rant on about something on the news that had set her off, and to excuse himself and be gone.

Back in the hall, Manny spotted Wayne standing in front of Tiffany's door, so he decided to take the back staircase, hoping that, on his way, Wayne might say something

"Hey there, Manny, what's up?"

"Nothing much. Same old. And you? You've met our new neighbor?"

"Yes, already." He smiled salaciously. "She's a charmer, isn't she?"

"You think so?"

"A lover of life type. Did you know, Encore may have its own in-house masseuse?"

"Oh?"

Wayne chuckled. "I met her the other day, and we talked. She gives massages, I almost went for one, my aching back." He grinned. "It aches on special occasions, like on that day."

Manny had to be civil, at least. "And did you?"

Wayne fell to a whisper. "Melissa was home. I couldn't risk it."

Wayne enjoyed digging it in, spilling dirt on another tenant, for he knew of Manny's discontent with the noise that he and Melissa made in their unit. Here was a chance to make himself and his girlfriend look not so bad.

"Very interesting," said Manny. Does she charge?"

"That's a good question. I wonder if she has a license to practice."

Manny grinned. "Nobody in this town has a license to do anything but kill."

Wayne gave Manny's line the laugh it deserved. "Rather convenient, a good back rub and maybe more, just across the hall!"

"Good to know," said Manny, walking away.

"You might give her a try, yourself."

Manny felt ignorantly insulted. Downstairs, he knocked on April's door. She opened it.

"Got something on our new renter."

"You do? Come in. I've got hot water on the stove."

Manny took his usual seat.

"So, please, tell me all about it!"

They had fun tossing the news around.

"So what do we do with it, Scotland Yard?"

"She may be charging," he guessed.

"And that's prostitution?"

"What else? Strange, looking back, I never quite felt right about her application."

"Are you kidding? You treated it like you were her agent."

"Oh, I did?"

April rolled her eyes. "And what now?"

"Well, that was then, maybe."

The two exchanged similar unspoken thoughts.

April said, "You're thinking?"

"A little poke about."

April grinned. "I could read your mind. And you're thinking?"

"Leaky faucet."

"Too soon for me to get out my plumber's wardrobe. We wait for more."

"Yes, I suppose," said Manny, then changing the subject. "You've looked a little down, April."

"Oh, could you tell?"

"It's about him?"

"Yes, you are right again."

April told Manny about her date on the grass with Jerry, and all the time he spent talking up his new Russian girlfriend.

"And you listened?"

"That I did, just like a friend should."

"Well, I'm proud. You scored more points than you know."

"I'm afraid I'm jealous."

"Of course, a natural feeling. After all, you're the one who held out for friendship, and that's the smartest way to start." He grew serious. "This modern play-and-lay scene gets me down. I'd hate to be growing up in it. I think about my late wife back in Melbourne, now there was a pal. And I wonder why she had to die, and it keeps me going. In some ways, I can feel her stronger now than when she was alive."

"You were lucky."

"Oh, indeed, I was," said Manny, taking another sip of tea. "Indeed, I was. Take it from me, when you've known what I've known, it doesn't die, ever."

He looked into April's eyes like a father giving advice. "It runs deep. And if that's what you want, your best friend is time. Time, if you respect it, can work wonders."

When Thursday morning was wide awake, Troy was still half-asleep on a skimpy floor mattress. The bright sun was arching over stage left through the window. Pulling himself out of a hangover in the small room he shared with the kid, Troy remembered leaving a message on Tiffany's answering machine — was it the night before? — promising to call her. Shit, what the hell was I thinking? He wiped some red off his face, dried blood. Where was that from? Oh, did somebody pick a fight with me in the Valley? He looked around. The kid was gone. I'm getting the hell away from this place, piss it off, and call Tiffany up and apologize, whether I promised anything or not. What time is it? Stand up,

Troy. Open your eyes and stare at one thing. He had survived another night in Hollywood's netherworld, being periodically awakened by nonstop disco drumming in through, it seemed, a thousand walls — or was it a bad dream? At one point, it sounded like Chic singing Yowsa Yowsa Yowsa, non-stop.

No breakfast from the kid. He pushed into his clothes, pushed up onto his feet, wanted to be anywhere but here. Opened the door and stumbled out, teetered down the squeaky hall and down the grumpy steps.

Out on Hollywood Boulevard, he would kill time in cheap movie houses, in bookstores, and then try his luck down where Tiffany lived on Encore Avenue. He had a hundred dollars in his wallet from half a night with Deborah, determined to hang onto it so that he, not Tiffany, would be picking up the tab if they went out. *If.* He should write a poem called If. If you were stiff, I would be softer. If you were soft, I would be stiff. Garbage, he mumbled to himself, in a fit of self-rejection. But a start, anyway. How he wanted to treat Tiffany like a lady. How he longed to appreciate her more, after having been beaten up by a rough and tumble "boyfriend" of Deborah's. Somebody who worked or hung around the place must have tipped off the thug about his having a new rival. One visit was okay, but a second wrought a bloody warning. His nose.

Now he remembered it all. Two brainless brutes had followed the car bringing Troy back from the valley in the middle of a half-night gig, back to Hollywood, and, once Troy had slipped into the lobby of the building, the pair followed him up to the apartment, jammed their way in just as he was entering, and knocked him around, only a little. "This time," they said. "Fair warning, guy." And after they were done with him and on their way out, one of them yelled, "Don't mess around with non-union actors."

He pulled himself together, had a little something to eat, and went out onto the Boulevard, to lose himself in a porno house. To store in his mind an image of the sexiest woman in the film. By late afternoon, he was strolling the grounds of the County Art Museum, which included the La Brea tar pits. He wondered why people made such a fuss over a small shiny pond of black tar surrounded by grass. Is this all there is? The elephant standing in it looked like it was on loan from Disneyland. Where were the big dinosaur bones? He saw a scrabble of what might be taken for bones, but barely larger than twigs. No wonder you didn't' have to pay to visit this joke attraction.

Bored, he resumed walking around the area, looking for Encore Avenue. He had asked a couple of people, but neither knew where it was. He came upon Springdale Way. He liked the name. And he took to the pleasant neighborhood, less starchy than the one in Westwood. Well-kept houses framed prolifically in flowers and ferns. He passed a large estate-like house set back beyond a great open lawn. And then a white building that seemed out of place, and more houses. At the corner, he went up to a man crossing the street.

"Sir, I'm looking for Encore Avenue. Do you know where it might be?"

"Encore Avenue," said the fellow, thinking in earnest. "Never heard of such a street, not around here."

"Well, thanks anyway," said Troy, continuing on.

"Hey, wait!" called out the man to Troy, now half way across the street. "Do you mean Encore Apartments?"

"Encore Apartments?"

"Right down there, middle of the block, the side you're on, I think."

Troy's face brightened. "Thanks!"

He walked down Springdale. Maybe it was the white building that he had passed on his way up. There was no signage on it.

A few steps further ...

*Encore Apartments.*

His heart stopped. Maybe close now! He was thinking of the body of the stripper in the porno film.

So this is where she lives? The older facade with art deco lettering gave Troy a better feeling. He could see his New York friend fitting in here.

He walked up to the front door. He studied the mail boxes, scanning strips of papers wedged in each, some bearing names, a few blank. T. Orr. Her.

A drumbeat of fear rattled his confidence. At the same time, the quality of their times together hanging out in Village coffee houses and talking poetry energized him. He felt the beat of New

York in his bones. They had shared it so well, like sister and brother. And here was that beat again—so close!

Tiffany Orr.

At last. Journey's end. No, a new beginning. Yes, Troy, a new beginning — at least for today.

Dare he try ringing her bell? He stood there, conflicted. He could tell her that Steve had given him the address, Encore Apartments. That's easy enough. She could only turn him away with some fuzzy excuse, but would she dare? He placed his index finger on the buzzer for T. Orr, and pushed it. And waited for a release buzzer to sound.

Nothing.

He tried pushing the door open. And it opened. She must not be home, he assumed, thinking he could leave a message under her door. There was a small table at the foot of a staircase. He pulled out a small paper pad and a pen, and wrote out a note, "Tiff, Surprise! I just dropped by. Got your whereabouts from Steve. Try you later. Troy."

And then, he walked down the hall, looking for her number. She must live upstairs. He went back to the front, and as he was on his way up the staircase, he ran into Jarred coming down, and what a find. Jared was clad in a taut black tank top giving his lithe, finely-toned body the illusion of nudity, and bearing in his smooth gleaming arms a basket of laundry. The lonely Jarred was stopped by Troy's exceptional looks.

"Hi, guy," he said. "Looking for somebody?"

Troy felt an unexpected rise. Only a male thing, he told himself, one guy admiring the assets of another.

"Oh, ah friend of mine, Tiffany."

"Oh, yeah, the new tenant upstairs?"

"I guess I missed her. I was going to leave a note."

"Yes, sure," said Jared, hoping to prolong the encounter. "Are you expecting her back soon?"

"I was just in the area. Thought I'd drop by."

"Hey, if you want to wait around a while, I'm going to the laundry room. There's chairs and magazines in there." Troy smiled.

"I'm Jarred."

"I'm Troy."

They shook hands with pleasure, each feeling a charge. Troy, slipping the note intended for Tiffany into his pocket, followed Jarred to the far end of the hall, feeling high on the vibes.

# CHAPTER 11

Tiffany was late getting home on Thursday. The clock said six twenty. She hurried to check the phone machine. The red light was not on. Nobody had called. What a letdown. But, in Troy's world, it was still early. Feeling anxious, wanting to be prepared for whatever the evening might bring, she transferred her compact frame into a casual skirt and blouse, hurried to the mirror to work on her hair and apply fresh makeup, and to paint her lips in deep red. She knew that Troy went for deep red, or that's what he told her in one of his more responsive moods. She had kept an obsessively detailed diary of those nights. Future screenplay. Warner will grab. And if they don't, she'll add a little more blood and pitch it to Universal.

She looked around the room. The bed was down, and that's where she intended it to stay. Since he had not called the night before as promised, it was likely he would this evening. A stand-up from Troy usually turned out to be a prelude to a come-through, one or two days hence. And this time, when he called, she would have to answer. No matter what she heard or felt, she would have to pick up the phone and speak to him and face the music.

The phone rang. She jumped. She was not going to ignore it

anymore. In fact, the more persistent he were, the more excited she became.

"Hello."

"You're there?"

"Is this ..."

"Yeah, me."

"Me as in" ...

"Troy."

"Troy!"

"I came by looking for you. Your friend Steve put me on to Encore Apartments."

"Yes, he told me you had called."

"So, at last, I find you at home, Tiffany."

He laughed, a little nervously."

"Yes, at last! How did you get Steve's number?"

"From somebody at your old Westwood address."

"Maureen?"

"Maureen," repeated Steve, thinking. "No. Joyce."

"Joyce?"

"She lives in the same complex."

Tiffany remembered a dreary young woman aging fast, in her thirties, who held down a government job. "Oh, yes, I think I know who that is."

"She's something else."

Tiffany asked, "Where are you now?"

"Right down the hall."

"What hall?"

"The hall on the floor where you live!"

Tiffany felt confused, diminished. What on earth was he doing down the hall? This was the Troy she had to share with others. The Troy she could never quite pin down. The Troy who drove her crazy.

"You're kidding? Is there a payphone in here?"

"I'm in your neighbor, Jared's place."

"Jared?"

"Only a few doors away from you."

"Oh, yes, Jared. Do you know him?"

"No, I was on my way up, about to slip a note under your door. Jared was coming down the stairs with his laundry, and invited me to hang out with him by the washing machines. Now, he's been letting me wait here in his apartment until you get home."

Don't lose it, Tiffany swore, consumed too soon and far too early with another distracting grudge. But Troy sounded so pleased with Jared's hospitality. She did not handle jealousy well.

"So, yes. Are you coming by?"

"Well, Tiff, that's what I had in mind to begin with."

"I'm just up the hall."

"Right. I think I can find you. I'll try. Give me, say, oh, about ten seconds?"

Tiffany forced a laugh.

"Barring traffic jams?"

Or Jared getting his hands on Troy before he's even out the door, dreaded Tiffany.

He breeze out, "See you, in a jiff, Tiff!" And hung up. Tiffany imagined Jared having cruised the life out of her New York heartthrob. And what now might she get from him? Leftovers? Get a grip, Tiffany!, she told herself. He's on his way to see you. That's enough!

A knock on the door. God, she prayed, feeling like Maria on her return to the Von Trapp household, let the music once more be alive for me!

She opened the door.

On this night, God answered desperate prayers.

There he stood, stunningly composed. So agonizing a symbol of a physical beauty no one person could ever possess exclusively.

"Troy, at last!"

"Took some time, didn't it," he said, stepping inside, looking around and trying to conceal a feeling of being let down. He knew what to say. "Beats your place in the Village."

"You think so?"

"Nice mellow neighborhood."

"Anyway, you're here!"

"I am," he smiled, his expression then changing when he glanced upon the bed.

"It folds into the wall," she explained. "But I usually leave it there, easier".

He said nothing in response. Was this his way of sending her a message?

She said, "Rest your feet, stranger, or look around. Have some fresh vegetables! Take a shower!"

"I might do that, Tiffany."

"And, how about a great big hug?"

Troy drew close. They threw their arms around each other, and held the feeling for a few moments. Troy let go, and walked around the bed, back to the little desk under the window with Tiffany's typewriter atop it.

"Anything new?"

"Still working on my screenplay." She always spoke of "working" on her writing, even when she wasn't. "A young director likes it."

"Really?"

"I met him at a workshop out near UCLA. He made some smart suggestions. I'm doing rewrites."

"Awesome," said Troy, wondering if the director was for real. Tiffany had banked her dreams on a series of so-called producers and directors who turned out to be all talk and no action. He sat down in the chair, inserted a sheet of blank paper around the roller, and wiggled his fingers across the keys.

"I'll fix us something to eat. What are you in the mood for?"

"Oh, whatever you're in the mood for," he answered, smiling to himself. She'll like the way I phrased that, he thought. She wondered if he was on some kind of sedative.

Tiffany slipped through the door to the kitchen to fix a plate of veggies, cheese, and crackers.

Troy looked over the typewriter, out through the window.

"What goes on in that building down there?"

"I'm not sure!" called Tiffany from the kitchen. And then she came into the room with some dishware to set on the table.

"Looks like a lab. Or maybe the home office of See's Candy?"

"White, yes!" Tiffany was amused, and returned to the kitchen in high spirits, calling back as she went, "Coffee or tea?"

"Coffee. Black!"

"Black." The word rippled up and down her spine like a thieving snake. Jared.

"Sugar?"

"Yes!"

He strolled towards the bed and gazed upon it. He studied the room's frugal contents, feeling unimpressed. He sampled the arm chair, and waited there in placid surrender, his mind comparing the bare furnishings to the artful decor of Jared's one bedroom down the hall, so different as to seem from another, more privileged world.

She returned with the tray of fresh vegetables, crackers and cheese, and set it down on the small table, to which Troy reported.

"Once a veggie, always," he said, sitting down into one of the three chairs at the table.

"And you," asked Tiffany. "Still binging on cheeseburgers?"

"Now, hot dogs, too."

"You tried the famous Pinks up the street?"

"Once, and I'm going back," said Troy. "Great little dive, all the photos of those stars. Not very far from here, either."

"Yes, I know," she said, feeling wonderfully reconnected to her ultimate Troy fantasy, and taking another seat at the table. She would not press him on poetry, not until the right moment came along.

He glanced her way with admiring respect, superimposing the body of the porno queen in the movie he had seen earlier in the day onto that of his modestly endowed host. "California suits you."

"You think so?"

"I think so. And, how are you getting by?"

"Barely," she answered. "I'm answering phones and typing for a private eye. He's basically a jerk, but they all are. At least, he's a flexible jerk. And he can be very funny."

"Oh?"

Troy looked around. "So, where's your LPs?"

"I didn't bring them with me. They're still at Francine's in the Village."

Tiffany pointed to a small radio on a small night stand next to the bed. "I still have music." Troy rose from the table and crossed to the bed. He turned the radio on and moved the dial slowly, past acid rock, his choice, to something more middle of the road, deferring to Tiffany's preferences. Here they were, at last, face to face, but Troy was fighting a mental distraction of the fellow up the hall whom he had just met. Surprised at how taken he had been by the looks of a black man. Something new. There had been fleeting encounters before, drugs and solicitations. But nothing quite like this.

He gazed upon the bed, skeptically. "It folds up into the wall?"

"Yes," Tiffany said. "For me, it's easier most of the time to leave it down. Want some wine?"

"Thanks, yes I would like."

She sprang to her feet, to take their plates back to the kitchen. Troy followed her to the kitchen door, and studied her reasonably in-shape anatomy, wondering what at the moment it made him feel. At least, no noticeable body fat. He hated body fat. Deborah, by comparison, was a knockout to look at — but only from a certain distance. Long distance love?

He looked down on the typewriter in front of the window, looked out and noticed a man standing down there, looking up. Is he looking at me, Troy wondered. He couldn't recall seeing anybody following him down the street. He returned to the kitchen door, leaning against it, his shirt having freed itself from behind the belt line, the smooth rippling skin around his navel now visible.

"Interesting area."

"I think so," said Tiffany, coming out of the kitchen, with a bottle of wine and two wine glasses on a platter. "A good mix of people."

Troy followed her to the table, and they sat down, and proceeded to enjoy the wine.

"And I see you can do your laundry right here," said Troy. "I met the manager in the wash room. She's a gas."

"She is," agreed Tiffany.

Troy relaxed a little more. "Perfectly to the point. This makes an evening."

They faced each other over the small table, between conversations, passing glances, passing time. The mood felt comforting to both.

She raised the subject that had brought them together in the first place. "So, are you writing anything new these days?"

"Am I writing anything new? Always, but is anything I'm writing, writing me?"

"Oh, I'm sure it is," she offered. "Someday, many others may be writing you!"

"You were always my best fan — no, not fan, my angel."

Her face brightened. "Well, thank you."

After an easy exchange through more small talk laced with innuendo, the wine was beginning to cast a carnal spell over Troy's weakening mood, blurring out his distracting thoughts of Jared, turning his focus onto the female directly in his line of vision.

"You're getting tired" she said.

"Am I?"

Getting up from her chair, Tiffany crossed to the bathroom. "Lie down, Troy, if you need some rest."

She went into the bathroom, and closed the door.

Troy rose from the chair, feeling the wine's effect, tottered over to the bed, and flopped on top of it. He felt like he could sleep here for hours. What a far and wonderful cry from the crummy old room in the abandoned building where the kid lived.

A few minutes later, when Tiffany came out of the bathroom, she gazed upon his sleeping body, feeling a privileged possession of it. She went into the kitchen, to finish up on the dishes and give him a little more rest.

Having kept his eyes closed, Troy lay still for a few minutes, and fell into a sleep. And when he awoke, it felt as if more than a few minutes had passed. The room was darker. He could barely make things out. The lights had been dimmed, it appeared, or maybe it was getting late. And then he felt the mattress joggling and her body nudging up against his.

He lay there indifferently, smiling up at the ceiling with his eyes half shut, and started in on a new stream of words, speaking them out loud. "Where am I? Whose room do I thrill this night? And how will I be judged when the sun returns? Is that a poem I am writing? ... Tiffany?" She elevated her position next to him, and looked down upon him with a predatory grin. He felt a strange liberation. She would make it easier for him, as she had tried to before. Role reversal.

He kept his imagination working overtime to transform Tiffany's frugal anatomy into that of the porno queen.

"How's it sound ... the poem?"

"*Raw*," she answered.

"Good?"

"Just ... like ... you!"

Flaunting a yawn in teasing surrender, he rolled over onto his backside. She loosened the top button on his shirt.

He sighed, "All the words out there and how to arrange them on a piece of paper."

She fingered his bare flawless chest solicitously.

"Feels good," he moaned.

"It does?"

"Yes. It does."

Across his neck, her thin wandering fingers shimmered like a warm summer stream.

"Ahhh," he exhaled. "Do you still give the foot massage?"

"You'd like one, Troy?"

"Please."

She went to work on his toes. He was hers, for the moment. They were merging in some kind of another union.

She whispered, "So, do you feel comfortable in my new place?"

"I suppose. You could do a lot with it."

"I could, like how?"

"Have you seen the one down the hall?"

"Which one?"

"Oh, what's his name?"

Was he talking about Jared? Incensed over the presumed snub, Tiffany Orr pulled abruptly away and raised up over the bed, as if about to turn away.

"Where are you going?"

"You don't like this place, right?"

"Of course I do, Tiffany." He waved a hand limply in her direction. "Come back! I need you. Please?"

She gazed upon him as he ripped loose the rest of his shirt, moaning, "We can do it like you want."

Tonight he would try the normal way in, rather than, like the time in New York when she had been open to "trying" it the other way. If the normal course failed again, she would this time probably be more understanding — or horny — and give in to what Troy had defaulted to in New York. Anything to keep him for a night. To be able to parade him in public. But now she was seething inside over suspicious thoughts of Troy and Jared, of whatever might have gone on between the two, and of Troy's pitting her small studio against Jared's one bedroom. It made her feel like a cheap make-do substitute.

"Oh, Tiff, I'm here. Isn't that enough? You got me!"

The words hit Tiffany's ears like a carnival barker's come on. She flared up into a ball of anger, ditched the bed and stormed across the room to the typewriter, wanting to make a lot of noise on it and annoy him.

He looked up. Where was she?

"Come on, Tiffany. More feet, please? I'm writing a poem in my mind right now ... your fingers are touring my toes. I am earth, you, a warm wind. That's not down the hall. That's here." Tiffany hustled back, infatuation trumping fury, and her consenting fingers gave Troy the caressing attention he desired. He groaned like an easily pleased dog in heat, and produced more words. "Draws me in, pulls me up, there and here, fingers traveling north" ...

Suddenly, he shot up into a sitting position, startling Tiffany.

"And she wants more."

He shoved his arm around her and pulled her body alongside his, turning it to face the mattress subserviently. On with what you want!

Tiffany caved to his raw masculine advance, to his desperate default into aberrational lust. Screw the feminists, she thought, turning her anger into aggression. She knew of many sordid things feminists would do for lusting men. "Is this what you want, Troy?"

"I'll take what I want, which is what you want. You have what I want, as long as you have what I want."

Tiffany Orr's compact body shook with desire and fear — the two drivers of the human condition (maybe, yes, traced back to a Garden in the Bible), and desire won out, so she allowed him the other, publicly shamed road plundered by true "sinners." This way, she would have him — maybe. It felt darkly promising. He was pulling her skirt down and grasping for the nether region, and finding a way in. But she could not shake off a mounting jealousy. "Is this about Jared?"

"Jared who?"

"Your new black buddy down the hall?"

"Jealous already?"

"Is it really him?"
"No, now it's us."
"Him later?"
"After you kick me out?"

Kick him out. Yes, I could do that, she thought. But something about his ruthless manner, his crude choice of words off the street only emboldened her hateful submission. He was getting stronger where it counted, a good sign, and she was helping him extend his power, and he entered her, at last, as he had desperately entered her back in the Village — to hell with society and ancient bibles filled with fire and brimstone, she wanted to scream. He knew he had to work fast in fantasizing onto the body beneath him the mental image of the porno star in the movie. Knew he had only less than a minute, max, to hold the contrived image of Tiffany — a body, not exactly hers — and get in and stay hard, and reach release and get out before a disrupting vision of somebody screwed up his concentration, leaving him limp, dry. "Pull me in, baby!" he shouted, desperate to deliver.

She twisted and moaned on the springy mattress, trying to manipulate his shaft into its ultimate form and purpose.

"Yes!" he screamed, feeling genuinely masculine and wanting to force on her a physical lie that would work this time. And there, he would betray them both. And there, he would prove to himself that he was yes, not "bi" but straight. And there, the two would compound another stolen moment with Eros, in their pitiful masquerade.

But Jared up the hall would not go away. She could not quite compete with Troy's private thoughts of a black beauty. Could not control her exploding anger. "No!" She bolted against the man now riding her. "Get off me!" she screamed.

"What the hell?"
"No more, Troy. No more lies!"
"What are you saying?"
"You can do anything you like, with anybody."

She jumped up onto her feet.

"What's got into you?" he said
"You can always go down the hall for that!"
"Shit!" shouted Troy, jumping off the worn mattress, grabbing Tiffany, pulling her back onto it. "It's you, you, you. We can do

it! Don't stop now!" She rolled over defiantly, onto her backside, pushing her missionary side into his face.

"Go ahead, "she dared him. "Do it like a man/"

"Turn over!"

But this time, she refused. "Get off me," she yelled. "Go somewhere else. Back to Santa Monica. Up the fucking hall!"

"Bitch!"

He lunged upon her, grabbing her by the throat, tightening his grip, pushing her down into quivering submission. She felt as if they were back in the Village reliving a trauma. She fought to free herself, barely able to articulate, "you're ... choke ... me!"

He let go.

He watched her terrified face, indifferently. He got up off the bed, picked up his clothes, crossed to the chair and slipped back into them.

She sat up on the edge of what felt like a war zone, staring the other way.

He grabbed the wine bottle and threw it recklessly across the room, and it crashed into the window, causing it to splinter out a hole. He walked into the bathroom, closed the door behind him, slammed it shut, and presently a sink faucet ran. She rose to her feet, crossed to the table and sat down, waiting for him to come out and leave.

After a few minutes, he came out, stood there glaring in her direction, then slammed the bathroom door shut, went to the front door jerked it open and stormed out, not bothering to close it.

He stumbled down the hall past Jared's place, and paused, wanting to, but NO. He stood there in stormy indecision, and then decided he had better not knock, not now. He only hoped that Jared had not heard the ruckus he had caused.

## CHAPTER 12

She was alone once more. Deserted. Hollowed out. Free. Safe. Embarrassed. Self-implicating.

She went to the door to close it. There was now a broken window to explain away. What would she ever tell Manny and April? She sat down next to her new telephone, wanting to call Steven, and cried.

In haste, Manny was climbing up the stairs to the second floor. He had heard some suspicious noises from above and had assumed it to have been caused by Wayne and Melissa going at each other. On his way out the door, he had spotted an angry-looking male figure coming down the stairs and going out the front door. What was that all about?

Cecil Fanton stepped cautiously out into the hall, heaving heard a loud commotion through his wall. His record player followed him out with a melodic stream of old songs from old movies. Manny came walking up, shaking his head. He pointed to the Wayne and Melissa apartment. "Are those two up to it again, Cecil?"

"No, I don't think so, Manny." Cecil gestured to the apartment on his right.

"The new one?"

"That's where it was. I heard a big argument through my wall."

"How long ago?"

"Only a few minutes. She had somebody in there. Male, I'd guess. Things got out of control." His eyes flashed deviously.

"A little whoopee?"

"Oh, I love that song, yes!"

Manny shook his head. "So then, it quieted down?"

"There was a loud smashing sound. I ran to the eyehole in my door and looked out. But I didn't see anyone out in the hall."

Manny shrugged. "What's this world coming to."

"Rock and roll is driving it mad."

"You can say that again."

With a shrug, Manny turned and went down the hall and down the stairs. Cecil entertained himself on the music coming from his record player.

How your charms never miss

How I'd love another kiss

You're getting to be a habit with me

He stopped singing, struck by a brainstorm "Whoppee goes to war?" And he laughed. Heady with a sense of his superior virtues, Cecil Fanton danced outside his door, feeling free of a corrupt, amoral and, worst of all, totally tuneless society.

Every hug, every squeeze

I'll have seconds, if you please

Your filling my heart with honey, you bee!

That's the kind of scoring he would reintroduce to the world. He was on a mission, and what better place to advertise it than the City of Angels?

In the apartment next to Cecil's, Tiffany's calamitous evening was receding into the calm of another day. And when the morning came, it came with another sullen layer of dark sky. Even the sun seemed too displeased with what had happened in there to make an appearance so soon after.

Downstairs, however, whistling up a note of cheer was the music of April's old tea pot on the stove.

A familiar knock on her door added a welcome touch to the morning.

It was Manny, there to brief April on last night's big scene upstairs. "No, April, not them. Hate to say this, but the new one."

"You're kidding. Come in, Manny, I've got water heating up. Sit down and tell me all about it."

Manny eased himself into his favorite chair at the table, and felt empowered with new information. April placed a cup with tea bag and a saucer before him, flicked some crumbs away, and went back to the stove. "I'm all ears."

"She had somebody in there last night, bad news. A lot of noise, and a crashing sound of some sort. I think the bad news is gone now."

"Why did we let her in, Manny?"

"Good question, yes. Not even here a week."

April returned with hot water for Manny's cup, and sat down to join him.

Manny took a first sip. "I was taking a walk about the place when I heard something amiss. I assumed it to be produced by our most charming tenants."

April giggled, then frowned. "But it wasn't."

Manny told April what he had learned from Cecil. "Now, there's more, something I discovered on my own." Anything to bolster his Scotland Yard credentials. "This morning, on my walk about the place, out there in the alley I happened to look up, and discovered a crack in her window."

"Tiffany's?"

"Yes."

"Oh, no!" said April . "Another Wayne and Melissa on our hands?"

"Well, we know who Tiffany is. But we've yet to meet her Wayne."

April inflated with giggles.

Manny slapped his knee.

April remembered, "There's a fellow I saw in the laundry room yesterday, maybe a friend of Jared's. Looked like an actor or model type. I wonder ...."

"If that was her Wayne?"

"Yes. Did you get a glimpse of anybody like that around here, Manny?"

"Nothing."

April poured more water into Manny's cup. "Time to get out my tool box?"

Manny grinned. "You're thinking?"

"We may have to check out her plumbing."

"I'm thinking, maybe it malfunctioned when her guest was over to visit."

They rollicked on a good laugh.

April said, "We have every reason, now, to go up there."

"Indeed we do."

He mulled it over. "But if she should be there, we're acting on a complaint from below, a leak that may be coming from her bathroom."

"Nailed," said April. "Let's wait an hour. She should have gone to work by then, I hope."

"Me, too."

Manny was looking forward to another search and find mission with Nurse Watson. And he was struck by the warmest feeling: whatever became of his crush on Tiffany Orr? Short shelf life? A picture of Manny's late wife flickered radiantly through his devoted mind, and he felt settled. There. Yes, there was the reason.

He returned to his apartment in high form, feeling almost as if he had come ever-so-close to an affair, but had walked away before it had a chance to compromise his fidelity. Still faithful to his only true love.

April dialed up Jerry at his workplace, to tell him about the latest, an excuse, really, to reaffirm the date they had made to go skating up in the valley that evening.

Tiffany woke up too late to straighten away the mess before hurrying off to catch a bus for work. She took another look at the large crack in the window, wondering how she could explain it to management. She came up with a reason. Her friend from New York was a baseball fanatic who carried around with him a practice ball. And he got carried away. Would they ever buy that? She turned other ideas and came up with the obvious excuse: It must have been the stalking stranger from down below. She could blame it on his having tossed a rock at the window. She had seen him standing out there earlier in the day. It made perfect sense, yes!

Thinking of work, in haste she forced herself into a skimpy skirt and a thin blouse, hurried into the bathroom for makeup, hurried in reverse out the door, down the hall, down the steps, out through the front door. Only did Cecil spot her exit, through his door hole. Doesn't look bad at all, he thought. I wonder if she can sing. He went back to work at his typewriter, hammering out a new scene for Act II of his musical.

The phone rang, with news from Cecil's mother, that her sister had died, and that he, Cecil, would be receiving an inheritance from his adoring aunt in the amount of about one hundred thousand dollars.

Carefully, Cecil Fanton repressed his glee. Carefully, Cecil Fanton poured out magnified tones of grief over the death of his favorite aunt and over her having so lovingly remembered him. He almost managed to extract a semblance of tears, assisted by his mawkish acting skills.

The bearer of bad (and good) news was buying it. "Oh, dear," said his mother. "I understand. Cry if you wish. I'm here!"

"I'll get over it, mother, in time," he promised.

When the conversation ended, Cecil Fanton rose like a confident Dick Powell in makeup and costume, and danced about the room as if he were on a sound stage hoofing the song destined to revive the real Forty Second Street, Cecil's catchy "Grabbing the Great White Way."

The hour for the plumbing inspection of unit 11 had arrived. Manny was, promptly, at April's door, his knock awaiting her appearance. She came out looking quite professional, although not in the clothes of a plumber that she had joked about wearing.

They went upstairs and knocked on the door to Tiffany's studio, and waited. She did not answer. She was probably gone. They slowly unlocked the door, and paused ...

'Hello? ... Tiffany? Are you in there? It's April."

No reply.

April entered, followed by Manny, who closed the door behind them. The messed-up room looked like the site of a wild party left for somebody else to clean up. The bed was still down, the sheets and blankets in disarray, as much of them on the floor as on the mattress. Two wine glasses stood forlorn on a small table next to the arm chair. Left standing was an empty bottle of wine. Uneaten cheese and crackers lay dormant on a round plate. A red light on the phone machine was on.

Manny studied the scene like an ace detective. They poked about the premises. When Manny went to open the bathroom door, it would not open.

"Locked," he whispered.

"What?" said April. "Well, knock on it!"

Manny knocked, but there was no answer. He knocked again.

"If it's locked, Manny, somebody must be in there."

"That stands to reason." He raised his voice: "Hello! Anybody in there? It's Manny and April!"

"I don't hear a thing," said April. "Should we call the police?"

"A little too soon, my girl. Let's dig deeper, first. This old place was built in 1924.". He took a pocket knife from his pocket, opened the narrow blade, eased it through the door against the lock, and tried to jimmy the thing free.

Success.

The door opened.

Their heads nearly flew off, stretching to see who might be in there.

"Nobody." announced April.

Manny had been hoping for something more disturbing or dramatic. He shook his head. "Well, I'll be."

The phone rang. They hurried over to the answering machine to listen in.

"Oh, Tiffany, oh, Tiffany," said a young male voice. "It's me. Remember Troy? How do I begin? Shall I count my shameful ways under the influence? Would you even believe me?"

Noisy street voices polluted the call, and the connection failed.

Manny gave a knowing look, "There's suspect number one."

"So Troy is his name," guessed April.

"Lovely little circle of friends she has out there," said Manny.

April shrugged. "Now what have we gotten ourselves into?"

"Welcome to the reality of managing an apartment house."

"Why did we rent to Tiffany Orr."

"She may be okay," said Manny. "Just another woman groveling for love, I'm afraid. Educated women are no different.

Just to be with somebody. All these women's rights movements. Feminism. I am woman, hear me roar! And still, nothing seems to change. They roar, yes how they roar – for more. I think it's getting worse. Biology clings to our bones. Buy a new suit, a new dress, a new anything, and all we really do is cover up the same old prehistoric bones, programmed to multiply. Who's fooling who?"

April spotted a business card on one of the chairs, and reached down to pick it up. She showed it to Manny. "Ace Modeling Agency, with an address on Ivar."

He turned it over. On the back side, somebody had scribbled out "Troy" and an address on Vista Del Rio, the number barely visible. Also in handwriting, "old building."

Now, that's interesting," said April. "Vista Del Rio. Where is that?"

Manny thought. "Up off Hollywood Boulevard, I believe." He handed the card to April

"We should write it down," said April. You got a pen?"

Manny flicked a pen from of his shirt pocket, while April fetched a piece of newspaper out of a waste basket, and tore off an edge for Manny to write down the number. After that, she put the card back on the chair.

"Prime evidence. This could be big," predicted Manny in dramatic fashion.

April saw an amateur sleuth overplaying his hand. "For what? For the mystery of how a window got broken?" She let go a flurry of giggles.

Manny slapped his leg in merriment.

They both harbored the same irresistible thought: another ride in Manny's old Buick, to another fact-finding adventure in the bowels of Tinsel Town. But neither put it in words.

"You'll have to replace the glass. You can take it out of her security deposit when she leaves."

He studied the messy scene around the unmade pull-out bed.

April was not sure. "Shouldn't we approach her first? See what she has to say?"

"Of course. Give her a chance to explain." He gazed over the room with a mixture of sorrow and contempt. "Looks like somebody's streetcar named desire ran off the tracks."

That tickled April.

Manny half-howled, and then turned serious. "Sex is ..." He sighed ... "nobody's friend. And how abused it can be by the most sophisticated idiots. There ought to be a license to love."

"Are you kidding?"

"No, I'm not. Mandatory classroom instruction. Start 'em out early. What to look for. What to run from. How to say no and stick to it. Good luck on that! Examples of how not to be fooled. Tough honest talk."

"Impossible," April countered. "We're too far gone. We're liberated beyond repair."

"Look down upon this glorious mockery of romance," Manny said, staring in disdain at the bed and the surrounding accouterments of seduction. "The great American dream, there in tatters before your eyes. Romance on demand. Romance out of a bottle. Out of some clueless self-help manual. Off the tele — between those fawning pledge breaks. Romance 24/7, and if you don't buy it, you're a prude, a simpleton, an impotent moron, a certified loser."

He looked away. He had seen enough for now. "So, have we fixed the mysterious leak?"

"Yes, I do think we have," said April. "Now, we've got the cracked window to be professionally concerned about."

"That we do."

"So, what next, Manny?"

"A drive to the address on the back of that little card?"

"I'm thinking the same thing."

"Just a little drive around the area to scope things out, you know."

"Of course."

"So when do we go, nurse Watson?"

"How about, say, eleven?"

"I'll have the car purring at 10:45," pledged a reborn Manny.

"Great! Let's get out of here."

They left the unit and walked down the hall. A snappy old Broadway tune was playing inside Cecil's unit.

"That lad's got taste," said Manny.

"But, has he a future?"

"Maybe, with himself."

April giggled merrily as they descended the staircase.

Came ten forty-five. An ambivalent sun had finally snuck around and past a heavy gray haze, its virginal rays piercing brilliantly through to widen its embrace of the city. So, the last workday of the week — Friday — would go out with a shine. April was out standing on the front steps, hearing Manny's old Buick wheezing up the driveway. She was ready. She got inside and they drove off.

They decided to skip the tourist scene. Manny drove up to Sunset, made a right, and then a left on Vine, up to Hollywood. From there, he headed east. April was looking out the window for Vista Del Rio.

"There it is," said Manny.

The street was more like an alley than a street. Manny drove up to a cul-de-sac sheltered by old trees. Most of the parking spaces were taken.

April glanced at a forlorn structure, a few stories high, that looked like a forgotten ghost. "There's the old building," she said. "You think anybody lives here?"

"Might still be a few hold-outs," he surmised.

"Looks creepy!"

Manny made a face. "Real actors lived there in the old days. "

"So this may be where our rock-thrower lives."

"It all makes sense. Broken window. Modeling Agency card. A woman who works for a very private dick and gives foot massages on the side."

April grimaced. "It looks so deserted."

Manny said, "I see some rags up there in a window. But first, I gotta park this thing, April."

Unevenly parked automobiles looked like a line of pushy actors in a cattle call audition waiting for their turns to be seen and routinely turned away. Manny found an opening and wiggled his large beast up to the curb under a graying old tree, and shut off the groaning motor, which burped in relief. The two got out, and walked up to the front door.

"Spoooooky!" moaned April. "I feel like I'm on the Universal back lot tour."

"This is the real thing, my friend," said Manny. Or, as the Doors would say "this is the end, my friend."

"Talk about atmosphere."

They walked up to the front door. Manny strained to see through its stained glass windows.

"A squatter's paradise, I'll bet."

"Let's try going inside to squat about!" chirped April.

Manny pushed his frail weight against the door. It gave in and opened. "We're in luck. What was the number on that card, April?"

April took a note from her pocket. "303."

"Must be the third floor."

"The penthouse suite?" quipped April, giddy as a kid at the door of a forbidden castle.

They walked cautiously through the grungy lobby, semi-lost in thick, tired-looking shadows. Somewhere from above came the ragged sounds of rock music.

"Bingo!" sang. April. "Somebody lives here!"

Manny made a face. "If that's what you call living."

April started toward the staircase. "Shall we?"

"Do you see an elevator?"

April looked around. "No concierge in sight, Sherlock!"

The sound of a car rolling up into the circle, and stopping outside the front door stopped them in their tracks.

Moments later, a heavy-set man in a worn-down suit entered, nodded at Manny and April as he crossed to the staircase and climbed up it.

"Let's follow him," whispered Manny.

They trailed him for a distance up the stairs, and then up the next flight, and the next, reaching the third floor, where he turned into a hall and disappeared down it.

They hurried over to peer around the corner near a post decorated with fading Egyptian symbols, hoping to spot the man entering through a door. Manny spotted him just as he was slipping into a room near the end of the hall.

April whispered, "What do you think?"

"If that's number 303, it might link us to Ms. Orr's problem guest. Wait here," he said, and tip-toed up the thread bare carpet to check the number on the door just entered. 303. He stood against the wall, only footsteps away, listening intently for sounds from within. April heard footsteps coming up the stairs, and waved frantically to Manny. He returned in haste, just as a young scroungey kid, skinny and shirtless, was bolting to the top of the stairs, around the post and up the hall, passing Manny on his way.

"It's 303 alright," he said.

"Hear anything?"

"A little of your favorite bar music."

More footsteps on the ascent. The two amateur detectives crouched together behind the decorated post.

A female figure came into view at the top, looked around without noticing the two spies, and turned into the hall and proceeded up it, and turned off down another.

"Tiffany!" April whispered.

"You're kidding?"

"I swear. Let's follow!"

Manny balked. "We can't let her see us!"

"Just up a ways, Manny."

They walked up the hall until it turned into another, and stopped. They heard voices around the corner. A man's voice. "Yes, where you cast?"

"I'm a friend of Troy's."

"Hey Ruben, there's a woman out here for Troy!"

Punk's voice: "Who are you?"

"Tiffany Tarter."

"Oh, ah, yeah. Tarter. I heard of you. No, Troy's not here just now."

Tiffany's voice, "Could you please give him this?"

"What is it, a summons?"

"No, no. I'm a friend."

"He has a friend?"

She pushed, "He's living here now?"

"Yeah, he is. Come on in."

"Oh, no, I'm in a hurry, but thank you just the same."

April tensed. "We gotta get out of here before she spots us!"

They hurried in reverse to hide behind the Egyptian post. Ttiffany came back down the hall, and headed for the staircase without noticing them. Down it, she disappeared.

"Okay," said Manny. "Wait a few minutes, then we split."

They hovered for a few minutes, then hurried down the cranky staircase, each step being answered by a puff of disturbed dust.

Out the front door, they looked around. Tiffany was nowhere in sight. They breathed the fresh air, exulting in their discovery. A scrawny young blond kid rushed by them and into the building and scrambled up the stairs.

'Well, by deduction," announced Manny, "I'd say that one of them was Troy, the other Ruben."

"Doing what?"

"Maybe each other."

They reveled in a good laugh.

The air was tranquil. The sun was poking through.

"What next?" said April

"Look over by my car," said Manny.

Now parked next to Manny's Buick was the gleaming white Lincoln Continental. At the wheel sat a squatty looking up-to-no-good Italian type, munching slowly on some peanuts. The ominous sound of a gun went off. One shot only. Manny motioned April to follow him, up and around the far side of the building, into a narrow dirt path behind a tree.

"Good Lord," April cried. "What have we gotten ourselves into?"

"Shhhh."

The character whom they had followed into the building and up the stairs now came running out. The Lincoln was backing out to leave, and the man threw himself into the passenger's seat, and the Lincoln bolted up the alley and made a sharp left onto Hollywood Boulevard.

Manny and April hurried over to Manny's car, got inside, and he started it up into coughing cooperation—the perfect sound track for glorious dilapidations all around.

"I wonder if she spotted your car, Manny."

"I doubt it. She's never been in it."

Once they were on their way, they shared speculations. It seemed clear that Tiffany's caller of the previous night lived there. Likely, he dwelled among the city's low life. They wore themselves out in conjecture. They let some welcome silence into the car. April looked forward to an evening of sanity with Jerry, at the old-fashioned roller rink in the Valley, albeit serenaded by the likes of Madonna and Heatwave.

## CHAPTER 13

Tiffany came home early from work that Friday evening, to face the ruins of her bungled reunion. To face the symbolic futility of two empty wine glasses. To wonder if the Poetry Workshop information she had dropped off at Troy's place would ever reach him. To wonder exactly what was he doing up there. She came away with a mind full of dreadful street-scenarios to keep her awake half the night. And to make her feel, already, out of place and under suspicion in yet another apartment house. They are probably onto me. I'm bad news. What was I thinking? I should hole up in some dive off Hollywood Boulevard myself — maybe a room in that old building — and then, to hell with having to avoid this. Had he only not thrown whatever he had thrown at the window. Will it ever end?

She rehearsed her excuse about a rock having probably been launched by the mysterious driveway stalker. She went into the bathroom to check the bruise on her neck where Troy had grabbed her. It wasn't all that bad. She could cover it over with makeup, or wear something high. But in this weather?

The telephone rang. She waited for the beep, afraid to pick up.

Beep.

A young male voice came on. "This is Rusty, for Troy, if there is a Troy at this number. Please call me as soon as possible. Thanks."

And a hang up.

She wondered if Rusty was the scrawny kid at the apartment who had accepted her envelope for Troy. Was he Troy's type — *if* Troy were really gay? She had always pushed such unpleasant suspicions from her mind, especially because he had never given her reason to consider it his fate. The mind is a fantastic instrument of self-deception, and Tiffany Orr's was not immune to her own.

She cleared the stuff around the bed, lifted the mattress in resignation and pushed it back into the wall. Picked up bits of glass below the broken window, tossed them into the garbage. Decided she had better go down and tell April what had happened.

A gentle knock on the door. Nervously, she went over to peer through the hole, afraid it might be him. Relief, it was only the manager. Now was the time to come clean. She opened the door. "Hello, April! I was just on my way down to tell you — somebody, I think, threw something at the window."

"Yes, I noticed it this morning, on my walk, from outside."

"Do come in."

April stepped in, surprised at how much less messy the place now looked. "That's unfortunate," she said, going over to the window as if to be viewing the damage for the first time. "Yes." She sighed. "It's pretty much gone. We're going to have to replace it. Did you find a rock or something?"

Tiffany was thrown off by the question. If the thrown object had come from without, it would probably be somewhere in the room.

"I only heard a crash, April. You know, come to think of it, I didn't find anything. Maybe it hit and bounced off?"

"Hmm," replied a skeptical April, not at the moment feeling so chummy towards her new tenant. "Well, yes, I suppose. That might have happened."

"Would you like something to drink, April?"

"Oh, no thanks. I have more things to tend to."

"Of course."

"Any other strange sounds out there?"

"No. A friend and I were visiting, listening to music, getting caught up. He's just in from New York. And then ... that."

April played along, and were it not for the ruckus that had been heard, she might have bought the story completely. But she would, for now, give Tiffany Orr the benefit of going along with a possible fabrication. She shrugged. "There are loonies out there bent on making life miserable for the rest of us." She turned to leave. "Okay, I'll arrange to have a new window put in."

"Thank you so much."

"No problem," said April, depressed over the thought of now having two war zones on her hands. "Okay, Tiffany."

She walked to the door.

"You have a good day."

How suddenly formal and distant did April now sound to Tiffany.

"And you too," said Tiffany.

April made a polite exit.

Tiffany felt relieved and apprehensive. They are onto me.

The phone rang.

She took the call. "Hello?"

Muffled silence at the other end.

"Hello?" She waited some more.

Nothing.

Maybe him, she hoped, wanting to thank her for having dropped off the information about local poetry workshops at Rusty's place.

Nothing.

She hung up.

What am I doing? She felt an urge to call Steven. To talk to a real friend. Not a pretend friend-maybe-lover-I hope. She dialed Steve's number. The machine came on. How good to be hearing his voice.

Beep.

"Hi, Steve, just thought I would check in. I've got to come clean, and well, talk it out to somebody, and you are my best friend. I saw my poet friend, Troy, last night. Yes, the one you know as Tom. It seemed to be going good for a while. And then, it turned awful. And I am so embarrassed. I'll tell you about it when you call. I'm okay. Oh, by the way, the fellow down the hall, Jared, asked about you. Remember him from the night you moved me in? He's a sweet guy, and lonely, getting over a break-up. Well ..." She made a wistful sigh, taking solace in her caring about another friend's love life and wanting to play a constructive part ... "You never know. Depending upon how you feel, I would like to have you both over some evening. Bye." She put the phone down.

Thank God for the Stevens of the world.

That evening at the Sherman Square Roller Rink, April and Jerry were together on wheels, just as it opened, circling the floor to the pulsing sounds of Jackson's "Rock With You" and Evelyn Champagne King's "Shame," expressing themselves with the triumphal air of two lovers high on themselves. Hot steamy Los Angeles summer evenings could feel like a great big open-ended seduction chamber, inside or out. The heat made both options feel about the same. Inside the old roller rink, April was feeling a tinge of desire over the body flattering cut-off Jerry was wearing. It made her feel desired. They had survived the disastrous visit to his place after clubbing that night. She'd been able to give him advice on his new girlfriend without throwing a fit. And they were still talking. Actually, flirting a little.

"You skate like a flower in the breeze, April!" he shouted through the music.

The breezy flower scattered a gust of giggles into the steamy air.

"And you," said April, "are like a graceful hound!"

Jerry laughed. And they frolicked like a pair of kids showing off on wheels. One sped ahead of the other, weaving around and through other skaters. One might glide deviously off into a different direction. Come catch me! And they lost each other in the crowd. A few rounds later and Jerry would find his lost giggle girl.

Jerry's eyes flashed at the sight of a familiar figure entering the rink.

"That's her!" he exclaimed. "Misha! The one I told you about!"

He pointed to a small dark-haired woman bearing a shapely

anatomy, who had rolled through the door, already on skates, and was talking to another woman.

I can't believe it, April thought. How could he be so insensitive?

"I'll have to introduce you to her!"

April felt diminished comparing herself to the curvaceous vixen, who was now talking to the overly responsive fellow at the skate rental counter.

"Were you expecting to meet her here, Jerry?"

"No, I wasn't! I wouldn't do a thing like that to you!"

Jerry's quick reply cooled April's inner rage. Get a grip, she told herself. I am a woman who sometimes does *not* roar.

After they had circled the floor another time, Jerry shouted, "I'm going over to say hello!"

"Sure!" she said, continuing to skate and wishing the worst for Jerry as he rolled off to seek out his Russian tart.

April spotted Jerry's new heartthrob, still speaking — it looked more like flirting — to the fellow behind the skate counter. What a flirt, April pleasantly observed.

She tried releasing herself to the crowd at large, hoping to stir up a little counter jealousy in the baker boy. A hunk of an overdone gym-type Neanderthal whizzed closely around April, his head turning back to give her half an eye, as if to say: you can worship me if you want. No charge.

Not bad, she thought. Something to take my mind off Jerry and his scheming little Miss From Russia with Greed. She slowed her speed so that it would take less time for the fellow to make another round of the floor, and to maybe give her another look-over, and a longer one this time. But no, now he was showing off in the center of the floor, spinning clumsily and falling flat on his fanny. Not a pretty sight. April turned away to enjoy a private laugh. What a clod. The sudden disillusionment caused April to have a talk with herself: Why are you so pulled out of shape that you would go chasing after that? Jerry and you are *friends*, April. Yes, April, she agreed. But, where has my friend gone? She looked around. He was nowhere in sight. Let him be.

A few more records played, and she spotted Jerry up in the refreshments area, sitting at a table next to his Misha, the two talking away. She felt a threat to her self-imposed composure.

"Shame!" sang Evelyn Champagne King. Yes. shame on them, April thought. The lights dimmed, throwing the floor into near darkness.

"Couples can skate," announced the DJ. "Solos, too." This was the new world order. No longer did roller rinks feature "Couples Only." No longer would wallflowers on wheels have to hide out in shame as the paired victors rolled smugly by.

Jerry tapped April. Standing next to him was his new flame, giving April a small smile.

"This is Misha, April."

"Hi, Misha! Nice to meet you!"

"Me, too," said Misha, checking April out with a fast glance over. The two women were so different — and yet neither close to thin, although the Russian clearly bore a superior anatomy.

I'll bet he's not giving *her* any pink boxes, thought April.

"April's my best friend, Misha."

"Nice to have best friend," said Misha, dismissively, flaunting her Russian accent.

April seethed inside. Why had Jerry fallen for this snooty little corkscrew? Why had he come on to me as if we were fated to meet? Fated to be this? She was losing control of her adherence to their friendship pact, wanting to rip it up and get real. She calmed herself a little by thinking that he was purposely keeping her stuffed with sugary donuts in order to minimize her attractiveness to other men.

"Are you two going to skate," said April. "Couples?"

Jerry put his arm around his new squeeze. The two young lovers glided off together. Oh, how utterly blissful, thought April, cursing his scheming corkscrew. She pleased herself with a self-serving scenario: Jerry is only doing this, I'll bet it was staged, just to make me so jealous that I will come around to what he really wants.

The theory helped calm her mind. And the music of Champagne King's Shame moved her, and she sang it out through the skating crowd, refusing to be depressed. Refusing to believe in Jerry and Misha. She isn't for him! And what a shame to have to go along with this charade. She would suffer it out. She and Jerry would be together long after that Russian corkscrew was either pimped into porno, or deported.

The brainless hunk was rolling past, flashing more dumb grins. He was alone and it was couples. Maybe he wants to skate with me? If he does, why doesn't he ask me? Oh, that's right, in here you don't ask, you just merge "into the moment," per the latest American self-help mantra for sexually desperate air heads. She started to skate out onto the floor, to butter up to the fellow. No, no, I might make a fool of myself, and they might see me getting rejected by a narcissistic nincompoop. Shame on me!

She rolled off of the shiny plastic-coated skating surface, and up onto the viewing area, and sat down on a bench, resolved to pull herself into herself, and watched the skaters twisting and turning to "MacArthur Park." When Jerry and Misha rolled past, April felt like marked-down merchandise at the Dollar Store.

She thought about other prospects: Arthur from Liverpool. Dashing, if pretentious. Money. I could use some. Too old. I could use some. Cecil? She laughed, almost out loud. But how special Jerry made her feel. She and he, instead of him and her out there, were dancing in her mind, dancing like they had up in the Valley in the boxy little club. She should be the one out there with him. They had come here together. Even as friends, she deserved more! Maybe Ms. Moscow had schemed to ruin their date. Already on skates when she entered — look at me! Maybe she'd heard Jerry mentioning something about going skating with me, and jealousy produced this obnoxious intrusion.

The music changed. The lights returned. "Couples" and "solos" were over. April wondered if "solos" meant people in love with themselves. She was up on her skates, hitting the floor with gusto, whirling in and out through the sweating mass in motion. Getting looks from men. Real men? Half the rink looked gay. So, let's see, if I say yes to Cecil's invitation for lunch — even Cecil now seemed a prospect. She noticed Jerry sitting on the sidelines with the object of his foolish desire, planting a kiss on her cheek, the two giggling away. Poor Jerry, she thought, wanting to believe he was being taken for a ride and would eventually come to his senses. Not just one kiss, but, God, another, and another, and — will they ever stop? How disgusting. To hell with him!

She skated faster through the moving crowd, producing a more animated version of herself. The hunky dude she had taken a liking to rolled up alongside her and mirrored her moves, and for a circle or two, they became a rolling spectacle of one-sided flirtation. She, playing the role, made a pass around his waist and brushed his backside, ever so faintly. But he only tolerated her pass, showing no reaction and refusing to reciprocate. I am no fag hag, said April to April, suddenly pulling away. Off the floor she rolled, noticing the absence now of Jerry and Misha, and wondering where they had gone. Had they missed her badgirl exhibition?

Jerry, she felt certain, would not leave without her. He had brought her here. April went to the snacks area and, beat down, gave in to her gluttony, ordering a Giant hot dog, Jumbo fries, Large Slurpy and a Double Chocolate Chip Cookie. She took her tray of happy food to a table and sat down to defiantly gulp it all away. She watched the skaters in the distance, not finding Jerry among the crowd. He will return, she promised herself. He has to return, to drive me home. They were probably making out in his car. Or back of a dumpster, shaming away.

About ten minutes passed, and he alone returned, still with his skates on. He found April in the snack area.

"Where have you been, Jerry?"

"Oh, Misha and I went out for some fresh air. It's so damn hot in here!"

"And where's Misha?"

Jerry's face shrunk. "I can't believe it."

How much easier was it now for April to be ever so sensitive: "It was going so well."

"That's what I thought."

"What about the hotel on Catalina. Did you ever talk about another one less expensive?"

Jerry looked beaten down by the fast lane of love. "We did. She said she would see if she could find another one she liked."

Another what, wondered April—hotel or man? Almost laughing, she kept the sarcasm to herself. She only said, "So?"

"I haven't said more about it yet."

"I hate seeing you this way."

Actually, she felt the very opposite.

Jerry opened up. "I never expected her to be here. Maybe she's the possessive type. She wanted to go outside for some fresh air. We skated out there. She said a girlfriend drove her here.

She sees this guy seated in his mansion on wheels, some foreign brand, with the window down, and she says she knows him. Tells me to wait, while she rolls over to say something. So I stand there, watching them talk. And they keep talking. And I'm starting to wonder, did she forget me? Then, I can't believe this — she is skating around the front of the car to other side, and getting in. She waves at me, wasn't that thoughtful? And the car drives off."

"Oh, I'm so sorry," said April, feeling gleeful inside.

"What a bummer."

"Did she know you were coming here?"

"I don't think she did. Maybe she heard me talking to somebody about it, maybe to you on the phone."

"And so she decides to show up, just like that?"

"Who knows."

The rolling Neanderthal rolled up to the concession counter, and actually showed some surprise when he noticed April sitting across the table from Jerry. When April looked up, he tossed her another leering grin. How smug she felt being seen with another man. Anyone but him.

April finished off her snack bar festival. Jerry suggested they go down and sit together on the padded bench overlooking the rink. April, feeling his depression, followed. She could now give him what he needed: comfort and affection. Manny would approve.

"I'm sorry, Jerry. It doesn't make sense. Many things don't, do they."

"She just shows up, tells me she is expecting to meet somebody here."

"So that was him in the car?"

"No. She didn't even know the guy in the car. He kept his eyes on her, so she claimed  Then she decided that maybe she did know him, from somewhere. She told me to wait while she went over to talk to him, that she'd be back shortly. Can you believe that? She leaves with a total stranger!"

Glowing inside, April sighed sympathetically, "I know the feeling."

Jerry put his arm around her, and she smiled contentedly, and they watched other skaters gliding by.

# CHAPTER 14

Later that night, Troy was out there somewhere on sketchy Hollywood streets, having thrown off the idea of paying Deborah another visit and risk getting beaten up again by her hoodlum harem. One bloody nose was enough . Even were he to accept her offer to serve as a live-in security guard — the promised pay very good and with no strings attached — he would still be taking a big risk. Like, he thought: what if, with me being armed, I shoot a gun off at the wrong hoodlum? Say, by mistake, at an intruder who is not that at all, but a boyfriend with an extra key to the back door? He did not like guns. He grew skittish around them. He had witnessed too many horrible things happen because of them. No way, he resolved, would he fall for Deborah's veiled proposition.

The streets and his freedom on them could feel excitingly fresh. And it made him think of Tiffany, who was, likewise, a free spirit, but he felt too ashamed of what had happened at her place to try making up so soon.

He had turned down the offer to be in a skin flick. Screw the idea of his being seen in sleazy movie houses, nationwide   He would continue to be his own man. He crossed Fairfax and walked east on Santa Monica, chaffing over the shallow scene in his mind but lusting after the easy money it could bring him. This was not really his world, and it never would be. He swore to that! He was thinking of Tiffany, of the poetry workshops information she had dropped off at Rusty's place, wondering when and how to approach her again. Another phone call in a day or two. Thank God he had not succeeded in choking the life out of her. Thank God he had let go, I'm learning to control myself, he realized, and he had shown the good sense to leave her apartment before he did anything worse. He was already practicing the words he would use in his next message. "I was so excited to see you. I got carried away. Shit, I was drunk!" That's what he could easily say — or did I already call her and say that to her machine? He could not remember.

How convenient was the excuse of alcohol for countless stupidities of lust. He would promise Tiffany a new sobriety. No drinks next time! He would lie, and then lie his way into, if not completely through, another reconciliation. She would understand. She would have to in order to have him back. That some women let him play them like cheap violins did not enhance his ambivalent regard for the female class of predator.

He burped at a passing car, burped because it slowed but then accelerated past him, and with his lips mouthed, go screw yourself, sucker! I'm not one of you! But there he was, down to only ten lousy dollars in his sorry-ass pocket, and he had promised Rusty a hundred of them tonight towards the free space Rusty had been giving him. He had, a pair of lucky nights before, smoothly bonded with a drug dealer, another native New Yorker who recognized Troy, and who had talked up the idea of their working the streets of East Hollywood, away from the hustling corridors. But then, he had lost the dude's phone number.

Troy's troubled police record included, among other more serious charges he habitually struck from his mind, and from Tiffany, his having spent a few nights behind bars for pushing dope and speed. He had broken those bad habits, long enough to land a job in a warehouse and soon become uncomfortable with the repetitive grind and with having to listen to his boring coworkers talking about their boring lives. After that, he had gone clean for a woman, much older, like Tiff, who helped him straighten up his act. Less than a year later, giving up on ever having a full relationship with Troy, she married another man, and the two moved away. Troy was once again left alone on the streets. He started writing poetry.

Now, he was out another night walking a few blocks one way, and then back the other, in search of fast and easy revenue — screw low-paying jobs flipping burgers! — unable to factor out the lucrative payoffs working Santa Monica Boulevard. At La Brea, he was waiting for another automobile to slow down and open up and pull him away from himself, into whatever he might be talked into doing, if the driver agreed to his price. Troy rarely negotiated. That was the easiest way. The startup interviews were brief, no references needed. The selling point was never to look desperate, but to be indifferent. Troy could do that well.

A car was slowing down to match his languid amble towards Highland. Troy glanced over his shoulder. The car was pulling up near a bus stop. The clue. Troy slowly walked over to the car. The driver was opening the passenger's door to say something.

Troy flashed a smoldering smile.

The driver asked him if he would like a ride.

Troy said he needed to raise some money.

The driver asked how much.

Troy gauged the degree of desire in the stranger's eyes and factored in his looks. Homely, out of shape – price hike for both.

Eighty.

The driver signaled yes.

Troy got in. They drove off.

Twenty minutes later, Troy was back on the streets, his confidence high, too too high for his own good. His killer stride was on a roll. He owned this pushover town! It was getting desperately late, the dark lights going darker. He'll get more.

Too late in L.A. can rough you up, toss you off your delusional path of easy-living, and throw you into cuffs or under nasty parked cars, the drivers unhappy with your promised performance. And you may hope to God you can crawl out, up onto the sidewalk before the auto shrieks away in disdain. They are not you! They live in Arcadia or Eagle Rock, or — what's that place? Gardena. You have messed with the wrong person, trying to con somebody who conned you right back, into the gutter. Get out of there, slide over closer to the curb, move your hands up onto it and cling and squeeze, until you feel your sorry ass being relocated onto hard cement in the middle of a penniless night — so far — near enough, you hope, to that cheesy little donut joint there on the ugly corner; the blood on your face not being met with derision by your co-walkers. There will be somebody, maybe more than a single somebody, who will sense what you have just been through; they will be ready to go cool and commiserate, maybe offer to buy you coffee and donuts if you've been robbed. Even if you haven't. Share tales of violent eruptions from the Johns who drive in from the small upstanding family towns, drive in for a quick drive-by "release." Release also from the dead-end lives they live. The Johns who can't figure the hell out who they are or what they want —odd, a little like you, Troy?

Just a little?

The anxious takers who pick you up because they can't resist, and then, the moment they cream into volcanic relief and are assailed by the jackhammer of instant guilt, turn into angry repentant sinners, hating the very sight of you. Blaming you for leading them "astray." They would never have done it had you not been standing there playing bad boy ready to tease and please daddy casting a hungry gaze in through the window separating you out there from him at the wheel. You on the street, Troy, crossing, going which way? The car that just passed you, its driver, not bad looking, nodding out the clue, or the one over there at the stop sign, a neck turning with a jolt to size up your butt? Come on over! YES, you will do. YES, meet me now, just as soon as I can move this thing closer to the curb up there, just in front of the BMW.

This other Tinsel Town night, Dreamland's wicked other half so seclusively open to money and/or sex and/or drugs — is a doomed playground full of incomplete souls angling to sample their errant leanings just for a little while, in darkness on a lonely street where only people like they go — just the Johns and the rent boys.

You're up onto the sidewalk.

"Hey, dude, you okay?"

Troy looked up. There was a guy younger than he, built like a bullet and with spongy bleached hair, looking down with a hint of compassion.

"You're bleeding?"

"I'm okay," said Troy, the victim of trying to pull off a hundred-dollar blow without having to blow. Of thinking that the driver had looked so lonesome and warm-hearted, that he could ask for half the toll charge up front, before lowering his trousers to the driver's anxious needs. Turned out, once inside the car, that he did not like the man's worn middle class looks. They reminded him of his own uncle in Indianapolis, whom he had always suspected. The closer he got to going ahead with the proposition, the more repulsed he became. As if he were actually facing his uncle up some anonymous alley. He would grab the first fifty, beg off for "just a moment" to take a piss (the best excuse, for the John would not want to end up with a mouthful of yellow instead of white) or to get coffee.

A large flabby hand covered the would-be poet's head, pulling it closer to the owner of the hand's crotch.

"I'm not doing you, kid. You're doing me, and I don't need to take a piss. I need for you to do me."

The image of it all, the imagined taste, horrified Troy, who'd never handled it this way, or so he insisted to his peers, although this wasn't the first time for a John to expect it of him. No, no, he wouldn't do it now, he had his limits — his standards — his male preferences — hell, his self-respect! — not for a thousand, well — maybe. The Deborah security-guard offer flashed favorably through his mind.

He pulled away from the driver and reached for the door.

The John grabbed his shoulder.

Troy was trying to push the door open.

"Do me or else, bitch!"

Before he knew it, John was being kicked in the groin and then in the eye and blood was sliding down his face. He had the door open and was trying to push the driver off of him, grabbing the driver's head and slamming it onto the wheel, and crawling out through the opening in the door, and falling into the street.

He lay there in a daze, disoriented, out of breath. He heard the car gunning up. He wiggled himself closer to the curb.

He feared the man was going to drive over him. But the car backed off at an angle, and all he could hear was its motor gunning up and then fading away.

He was there alone in the street.

He told this to the young hustler who was looking down upon him

"Did he take your money, dude?"

Troy felt for his wallet.

"No."

"Here, can you get up. Feel any pain?"

Troy sat up on the sidewalk, rubbing his hand over the blood smears on his face

"I've seen you somewhere. I know, are you Rusty's friend?"

"Yes."

"Rusty likes you. Here, let me help you to the bathroom down at the donut place," said the kid.

"Thanks," sighed Troy, believing that in Rusty there still might be a friend — hoping the kid had really liked him and was not just pimping for some two-bit flesh flick operation. They all usually wanted more. Nobody really wanted a friend. If they did, as soon as money came along, the friend was put on hold. Troy hated being put on hold.

The deepening night seemed to stand stony still. As if God had declared an intermission, a time out. Everybody behave yourself for a few perfectly harmless hours! One cruising cycle had ended as another night of insatiable thrills was slipping away, like sludge down rat-infested drain pipes, vanishing into silent remorse and into a settled comforting quiet, neither barren of hope nor riddled with strangers consuming strangers. Just at the fragile break of dawn did the city beam, once again, with fresh promise and with an illusory innocence as wonderfully embracing as an old movie musical.

Saturday morning came with a soft smile of sunshine covering the filth and tears left over on desperately walked streets, and the town seemed bathed in the glow of nature. April called it a lazy Saturday sun taking the day off.

April heard Manny's distinctive knock on her door — a kind of password granting him guaranteed reception, except when she was not in the mood. The two respected each other's space. She got up and answered it.

"Morning, Manny! Please, please, no bad news."

"All quiet up there."

"Sit down and I'll make you a cup of tea."

"You and Jerry have anything planned for the day," asked Manny.

April frowned. "No, not as of this moment. I think he's too depressed over his Russian princess."

Manny chuckled. "They can be such heartless opportunists. It's probably about money and citizenship."

"I don't think Jerry has that much to dig. I'd hate to see his heart broken."

"I don't know." said Manny. "He may be embarrassed. You think he's really bothered that much?"

April turned inquisitive. "What are you saying?"

"I use my top to figure things out. He comes back into the rink, wins over your pity, sits down next to you and then – things turn warm and cozy. Am I right?"

"Might be," said April, wanting to change the subject with better news. "There's this other guy, I met him a few weeks ago, never told you about him. He's 20 years older than me."

"Twenty years," though Manny. "I'm not put off."

"From Liverpool."

"Oh, another English fellow. You do like them."

"Do I?"

"Never married?"

"Once. Now, he's getting a divorce, he says. Or claims."

"Still married." Manny looked down and away.

"Yes, I know, one of those. He does have a charming manner, and the way he talks! He called me last night after I got home from skating. We talked for over an hour."

Manny gaged a rare gleam on April's face.

"Gives you a tingle?"

"He does," she confessed.

"So," said Manny, changing the subject. "What about our broken window?"

"I talked to Alex. He said go ahead and have it replaced, and leave it at that. After all, there *was* a weird man out there on the driveway, like Tiffany said."

A sudden harsh knocking against the door. April got up to answer it, but first looked through the hole. "Talk about weird."

She opened it to greet the oddly charming Dudley Bufforn,

who lived in the unit on the far side of Tiffany's. A lumbering forty-five year old still-a-boy from upstairs, he worked in word processing at a law firm, and collected graphic comic books and sci-fi novels.

"Hey, April! Wayne shot Melissa dead last night during a late-night porno shoot at a roller rink!"

"Are you kidding?" She knew Dudley to be a prankster.

"It's on the news. Right now! He caught her up in the valley getting done by some big name stud! And on roller skates, ha! Pulled out a gun and shot her dead. Just a few hours ago. Inside a roller rink! Ha, those places are such greasy dives. I used to hang out in one. Wonder if they did it to old organ music?"

April grew excited thinking that it might have happened in the very same rink where she and Jerry had skated. And, maybe only a few hours after they had they left.

Dudley liked to lay it on for effect. "Ain't that a doozy! Police nabbed him on a car chase clear out to Malibu. He's now behind bars."

Manny's face froze in shock, and then, feeling professional relief, melted away into a lovely satisfaction.

At last. Fate had done what neither he nor April could do: evicted two problem tenants with the clean swift blow of three get-even bullets. Penetration guaranteed. One was dead and not from play acting, the other behind bars. Real bars. Not a good day for New Jersey.

Dudley ran off.

April was now seated in front of her television, waiting for the screen to produce a picture. The channel that came on was covering the murder. Encore Apartments got mentioned, too, and prominently. Pearl Dubuque's name played a starring role. No doubt, she was upstairs glued to her old RCA console color set, riveted to every word, planning to exploit the incident as the pretext for her next "imminent" return to the silver screen. She would have Mr. Cecil Fanton back to discuss his project, but after first touching bases with her connections at RKO and The Famous Lasky Players. No later than Monday morning would she be back into facial rehab.

Manny and April shared a rare feeling of bad-tenant elimination by default. Credit lust, jealousy, and revenge. And credit a little business card for a film company that had been slipped into a coat pocket of Wayne's while he was out and his studio was being entered, officially of course, for reasons having to do with a mysterious leak into somebody's unit below. Manny chuckled lightly to himself, thinking about it—his best business card referral in years

Manny and April found unspoken satisfaction in watching TV replays of a mad car chase culminating in Wayne being handcuffed at the edge of a swimming pool at a stately old mansion just above Sunset Boulevard. Encore Apartment's Scotland Yard division shared a sense of welcome irony: The murder made their new iffy renter upstairs seem not so iffy. For now at least. Maybe they had made the right decision after all.

One apartment down. Another on the watch list

# ABOUT THE AUTHOR

Entertainment writer Lewis Byrd has walked Hollywood's boulevards of glamour, its side streets of misfortune, poked up and down its darkest alleys, and called home in historic apartment houses teaming with starry-eyed dreamers and jaded has-beens, the old and the young intersecting in a frantic wonderland of ambition.

He knows the landscape inside and out — from the hard scrabble streets of East Hollywood to the lovely calm of Westwood on the west side.

With family roots in the film industry and his own tenure as a one-time resident and player, Byrd brings to every page an intimate knowledge of this mecca's collective infatuation with Tinsel Town fame. But here, he draws on the everyday lives of the millions who do not draw pay checks from Warner or Paramount.

Made in the USA
Columbia, SC
01 November 2018